B-1   6⁰⁰

This is my Book

Georgia Ina.

33/3 Kessler

Wichita Falls, Texas

FROM

DOT AND HER UNCLE WENT FROM TREE TO TREE EMPTYING
THE PAILS OF SAP

"Dot and Dash at the Maple Sugar Camp" (see page 102)

DOT AND DASH BOOKS

DOT AND DASH
AT THE
MAPLE SUGAR
CAMP

by

DOROTHY WEST

ILLUSTRATED

CUPPLES & LEON COMPANY
PUBLISHERS . . . NEW YORK

DOT AND DASH BOOKS

By Dorothy West

DOT AND DASH AT THE MAPLE SUGAR CAMP

DOT AND DASH AT HAPPY HOLLOW

DOT AND DASH IN THE NORTH WOODS

Other Titles in Preparation

CUPPLES & LEON COMPANY

PUBLISHERS . . . NEW YORK

CONTENTS

DOT AND DASH
at the
MAPLE SUGAR CAMP

CHAPTER I

A RIDE INTO THE COUNTRY

"LOOK out, Roger!" Dot called shrilly to her small friend who was skating on the Davidson's driveway. "Daddy wants to back his car out of the garage!"

"Oh, I'll get out of the way all right," the boy laughed. "I'm a fast skater. Just watch!"

Roger took several quick strokes and rolled down the driveway toward the street. The steep slope made the wheels of his skates whirl faster and faster. He suddenly lost his balance and fell down on the hard cement.

"Oh, Roger, did you hurt yourself?" Dot

1

asked anxiously as the little boy sat up and began to cry.

"I s-s-skinned my knees," Roger said between sobs.

Dot saw an ugly red spot on each of the little fellow's knees. She quickly unstrapped her own skates and helped Roger up. She guided him over to the lawn and left him sitting there while she ran to the garage to tell her father.

"Oh, Daddy," she called, "wait a minute. Roger is skinned."

Doctor Davidson looked down upon his little girl from behind the wheel of his big coupe. Then he lowered the glass of the window and asked gravely: "Where?"

"On his knees, Daddy. Both of his knees. Won't you please come and put some medicine on him?"

Doctor Davidson smiled broadly at Dot. Taking his black leather case from the car, he stepped down to the ground.

"Now where will I find the patient?" he asked.

"Right this way, Daddy," said Dot, slipping her small hand into his large one. "He's on the front lawn. He got skinned trying to show off."

When Roger saw Doctor Davidson coming with his black satchel he forgot all about his bruises and tried to get away. Roger was like a great many other small boys. He didn't like to take medicine. So when he saw Dot with her father he scrambled to his feet and tried to skate right over the grass. He took just one stroke and down he went.

"Don't act silly, Roger," Dot pleaded. "Daddy won't hurt you. He just wants to give you some medicine."

Roger held his hand over his mouth and shouted: "I don't want to take it! I don't want to take it!"

"Brave boys don't cry before they have been hurt," Doctor Davidson said kindly.

He looked at Roger's knees and then from his satchel took out a piece of cotton which he soaked in alcohol. He sponged off the little boy's wounds and painted them red from another bottle.

"See, it didn't hurt, did it, Roger?" Dot asked.

"No, it just stung," Roger answered. "Am I all cured now?"

"Well, I should say that you are well on the road to recovery," the doctor replied, smiling. "Let's see if you can skate."

He lifted the boy to his feet and carried him to the front sidewalk. Roger stroked carefully on one skate and then the other. It did not hurt so he skated faster and faster until he was out of sight down the street.

"Who are you going to cure next, Daddy?" Dot asked as she ran along at her father's side. He had picked up his black bag and was going back to the garage.

"Well, young lady, I am making a call upon Mrs. Graham out in the country."

"Oh, I know *her,*" Dot cried gaily. "Once you took me with you when you went there, Daddy! Don't you remember? She gave me some cookies with raisins in them. Take me this time too, won't you please, Daddy?"

Dot was excited now. She liked nothing better than to go with her father to call on his patients.

Doctor Davidson looked at his watch. "You may come along, Dorothy," he agreed, "but first you must ask your mother."

Dot ran into the house and called her mother's name. When there was no answer, she scampered down the basement steps to the laundry. Mrs. Davidson was helping the laundress wash lace curtains.

"Oh, Mother," Dot cried, out of breath from running. "Daddy says I may go with him if you say 'yes'. Please say it quick, Mother. He's waiting."

"Now you're all excited, dear," said Mrs. Davidson. "Be calm and tell Mother where you're going."

"Oh, just out to Mrs. Graham's house. She bakes raisin cookies when she isn't sick."

Dot's mother coughed to hide a smile. "I'll talk with your father," she said. "You may wait here with Mrs. Green for a few minutes."

Mother wiped her hands on a towel and went upstairs. Dot stood by a tub full of curtains and looked down upon the frothy suds. She was only six years old and barely could see over the edge of the high tub.

Mrs. Green gazed down at the blue eyed, curly haired little girl and smiled, for she was very fond of her. And Dot thought that Mrs. Green was a very fine lady too who could do nearly everything. She had been working in the doctor's family since long before Dot was born.

"What makes soap suds white, Mrs. Green?" Dot asked earnestly.

"My land, child! They're white just because they're white. What other color could they be?"

"Why aren't they brown? Isn't that bar of soap they come from brown?"

Mrs. Green put her elbows on her hips

and sighed. She liked to answer Dot's questions, but there were some she could not answer.

"I'm afraid Mrs. Davidson will have to explain that to you," she said. "Listen! I think I hear her calling you."

Dot ran up the stairs as fast as she could and met her mother coming from the garage.

"Oh, may I go, Mother?" she asked excitedly.

"Yes, dear, but you must wear your warm coat. This early spring weather is so changeable it may turn cold any minute."

Dot was the only child of Doctor and Mrs. Davidson and her mother was always thinking of her comfort. Yet the little girl was not in the least spoiled. She seemed to take a sensible view of things and always was glad to help her mother in any way she could.

Dot went to the hall closet for her heavy coat. And then she thought that she might be lonesome in the car while her father was making his call, so she ran upstairs to get one of her dolls. She hardly knew which one to take, but finally she chose Imogene, her favorite.

Holding the doll tightly, Dot climbed into the car with her Daddy, snuggling close beside him.

They drove along a maple shaded avenue and on to the main section of Fremont. Dot turned to glance at her father's office building where a black sign with gold letters read: "Frank L. Davidson, M.D."

"Does 'M.D.' mean Mr. Davidson?" Dot once asked her father.

"No, Dot," he had laughed, "it's just another way of writing 'Doctor.'"

It was a pleasant day for a drive into the country and the little girl saw many interesting things. After awhile they passed a herd of cows lying by the banks of a creek, chewing their cuds and looking lazy and contented.

"Daddy," Dot asked, "why do cows chew when they aren't eating?"

"A cow's stomach is different from ours,"

Doctor Davidson explained. "When a cow eats grass she just gulps it down without chewing it at all. The grass goes into one part of her stomach, then after a while it comes up again and she chews it fine, and it goes into another part of her stomach. When she does that, we say she is chewing her cud."

"How funny! But how can she keep from getting her stomachs mixed up?"

"Oh, Mother Nature takes care of that," the doctor replied.

Dot did not ask any more questions about the cows because she thought perhaps she had asked enough already. She sometimes wondered who 'Mother Nature' might be, but grown-ups knew so many things a little girl could not understand. Her father always was willing to explain matters to her the best he could, because Dot did not ask questions just to be talking. She really wanted to learn.

Before long they came to Mrs. Graham's house and Doctor Davidson parked the car on the driveway just off the main highway.

"I'll be back in a few minutes, Dot," he promised as he took his black bag and walked up to the house.

To amuse herself, Dot held Imogene up to the car window so she could see the sights. There was the big barn, the windmill, the orchard—in fact, so many wonderful things that Dot did not have time to show them all to her doll before her daddy came back. He was carrying a brown paper bag.

"Oh, Daddy!" Dot called. "What do you have in the sack?"

"Mrs. Graham sent you some cookies."

"Oh, thank you, Daddy—I mean her. Have they raisins in them?"

"I think so," her father replied as he gave her the sack. "Now only one, young lady."

He started the car and they rolled slowly out on the main highway.

"Are we going home now?" Dot asked between bites.

"That is what I am worrying about,"

said the doctor. "I just had a phone call to stop and see old Mr. Holloway. It will be a long visit I'm afraid and you may get very tired waiting."

"Aren't there any little children at Mr. Holloway's house? Maybe I could play with them."

"He hasn't any boys or girls. I would take you home but Mr. Holloway is a very sick man. I must go right away."

"I won't get tired, Daddy." Dot did not want to go home, even if she had to wait in the automobile for a long while.

"I might drop you off at Mrs. Harrison's."

"Oh, that would be just fine!" Dot cried. "Mrs. Harrison has two peacocks. Once she gave me a pretty feather."

As Dot and her father drew near the Harrison farm, they saw a large crowd of people there. The yard was jammed with automobiles. Farmers and their wives were grouped around the barn and other outbuildings.

"Why are so many people at Mrs. Harrison's place, Daddy?"

"I had forgotten," said her father. "This is the day of their auction sale. I'm afraid I'll have to take you with me after all."

Before he could drive away, a plump woman with a jolly, kind face came hurrying down the path. It was Mrs. Harrison.

"Good morning, Doctor," she beamed. "I hope Dot has come to pay me a visit."

"Daddy says I can't stay because you are having an auction sale."

"I'd not think of imposing upon your good nature, Mrs. Harrison," said Doctor Davidson.

"Dot won't be a bit of trouble," Mrs. Harrison declared warmly. She opened the door of the car and lifted her down. "We'll take good care of her until you get back, Doctor. We may decide to keep her for our own little girl," the woman concluded, a warm twinkle in her eyes.

Dot smiled up at Mrs. Harrison for she

knew the lady was only joking. So many people said the very same thing.

After the doctor had driven away, Dot and Mrs. Harrison walked toward the sales ground.

"What do people do at an auction sale?" the little girl asked as she watched the farmers milling about.

"What do they do? Why bless your heart, they come to buy things. That is, some of them do. Others stand around and talk, and a few, I'm afraid, are only interested in our free lunch."

Dot would have liked some lunch herself for the ride had made her very hungry. She remembered that it was not polite to hint for food.

"Would you like a nice beef sandwich, Dot?" Mrs. Harrison asked, for she seemed to understand about little girls and their big appetites.

"Oh, yes," Dot beamed. "I like sandwiches better than anything except ice cream."

Mrs. Harrison led her through the crowd to a large wooden stand where the counters were piled high with food. A man in a white apron handed them each a juicy hot beef sandwich. Dot thought she had never tasted anything quite so good.

Mrs. Harrison then walked with her about the sales yard, and she saw many things which were to be sold. There were wagons, horses, bridles, harness, household goods, chickens, turkeys, and most wonderful of all, Mrs. Harrison's prize peacocks.

As they paused in front of the pens, one of the birds suddenly spread out his beautiful tail like a fan. He strutted around as if to say: "Am I not marvelous? I would just like to see you match *that!*"

"Oh, Mrs. Harrison, are you going to sell these pretty peacocks?" Dot asked.

"We are selling everything," Mrs. Harrison explained. "You see, my husband and I have worked hard all these years. Now we have decided to sell the farm and move to town."

"Oh, I wish you would come to live on our street! And it would be nice to bring your peacocks. Then I could see them every day."

Mrs. Harrison smiled and shook her head. Peacocks were too much trouble, she explained. Besides, she would have no place for them in town. They must be sold.

"Peacocks wouldn't be too much trouble for *me*," Dot said. "I wish my Daddy were here! Maybe he would buy them for me."

"Where could you keep a peacock, child? They must have plenty of room in which to run."

That was a hard question. Where could she keep them? Grown-ups were always thinking of something like that to ask. Dot puckered her forehead and said: "Well, maybe in the garage."

"I'm afraid that wouldn't do at all," Mrs. Harrison answered. "But if your father is willing, I'll be glad to give you one of the peacocks."

"Oh, thank you!" Dot cried. "If you

don't care, I'll take the one with the brightest tail!''

"You may have either one you wish. That is, if your father gives his permission.''

Just then a man called to Mrs. Harrison. She explained to Dot that he was the auctioneer who was to sell their things.

"I must talk with him for a few minutes,'' she said. "You wait right here, dear. I won't be long.''

Dot sat down on an old box. Nearby were chairs and dressers and rolls of carpet. People walked to and fro looking at the furniture but after a while they heard the auctioneer shouting down by the barn:

"How much am I bid for this fine Jersey cow? Sixty! Sixty! Who will make it sixty-five?''

They knew then that the sale had started and hurried away so they would not miss any of it.

Dot was getting tired now. She wished that Mrs. Harrison would return. Just when she thought she would go and search for her, she heard a "yip, yip, yip," which seemed to come from directly behind her.

Dot sprang up and listened. She could not see a dog anywhere although it did sound exactly like one barking.

Then she noticed a large, wooden crate on the ground. Someone had dropped a piece of old carpet over the top slats and the sound seemed to come from underneath.

Dot pulled aside a corner of the carpet and there in the crate was an adorable little black and white fox terrier!

Dot reached in and petted him. The terrier wagged not only his tail but his whole body. He licked her hand and if Dot had not been watching, he would have stuck his nose through the slats and kissed her right in the face.

"Oh, you darling little dog," Dot laughed. "Who shut you up in this old pen?"

The dog gave another bark as if to tell her all about it.

"Oh, I wish you were mine," Dot said

wistfully, petting him again. "I know just what I would name you. I would call you DASH. How would you like that?"

The terrier gave two joyous little yips as if to say that he would like it a great deal. But just then a man walked toward Dot and she saw that he meant to pick up the box.

"Oh, you're not going to sell *him!*" she cried.

"Yes, little Miss," the man said kindly. "We must sell everything."

Dot looked down at her new found friend. Dash looked back and whined pitifully.

Then the man lifted the crate to his shoulder and carried it away.

CHAPTER II

DASH FINDS A HOME

MORE than anything in the world Dot wanted Dash for her very own. She didn't speak a word as the man lifted the box and carried it away, but she knew that somehow she *must* save the little dog.

Forgetting that she was to wait for Mrs. Harrison, Dot ran after the man. She easily caught up with him for the crate was so heavy that he could not walk fast. She could see poor Dash sliding back and forth in the box. Once she heard him whine.

The man set the crate down on the ground beside a stove which was to be sold. He did not appear to notice when Dot dropped down on her knees so that she could peer through the slats.

"Oh, you poor little doggie," she whispered.

When Dash saw his friend again he became greatly excited. He stood on his hind legs and scratched the box with his fore-paws. Then he looked up at Dot and his eyes seemed to say: "If only you would get me out of here, we two could have loads of fun together!"

The little girl saw that a large number of people were coming toward her. They formed in a large circle about the auctioneer as he stepped up to a kitchen stove beside Dash's pen.

"How much am I offered for this fine range?" he asked in a loud voice. "You will make no mistake in buying this stove. It is as good as it was the day it left the factory."

A lady held up her hand and said: "Ten dollars."

"Ten dollars for this fine stove. Who will make it twenty dollars? Bid up, ladies and gentlemen, bid up!"

As the auctioneer talked very rapidly, his eye roved toward the crate which held the fox terrier. Dot read the thought in his mind. He meant to sell the dog next.

The little girl knew she would have to do something right away. Perhaps Mrs. Harrison would give her Dash instead of the peacock! The bird would be a nice pet, but after all he was not a *person* like Dash. She would trade a dozen peacocks, if she had them, for a cunning dog.

Dot sprang to her feet and set out to find Mrs. Harrison. The kind lady was talking very earnestly to a farmer. Now Dot had been taught never to intrude upon grownups when they were busy, but she could not wait when Dash's future was at stake. Timidly she tugged at Mrs. Harrison's dress.

"What is it, Dorothy?" the woman asked.

"Please, Mrs. Harrison, it's about the peacock—"

"I am very busy just now," Mrs. Harrison said kindly. "We'll discuss it in just a minute."

Dot waited a little while but the talk went on and on. She was afraid Dash would be

for this fine smooth-haired Fox?" shouted the auctioneer.

No one spoke. Everyone seemed to be looking at Dot.

"Who will give three dollars?" asked the auctioneer impatiently. "Two dollars? One dollar?"

Still no one uttered a sound.

"The dog will be withdrawn from the sale," the man said. "I cannot sell a fine pet like this for twenty cents."

Just then Mrs. Harrison came hurrying through the crowd searching for Dot. The auctioneer stopped her and they whispered to each other for several minutes. Then the man nodded and faced the crowd again.

"I have been instructed to sell the dog for the price offered," he announced. "He is yours, little Miss, for twenty cents."

When Dot heard that Dash belonged to her, she scarcely could believe her ears. The crowd started to applaud. Folks smiled at her and clapped their hands because everyone was glad that Dot's bid had been accepted. She gathered up her money and gave it to a man who wrote her name and address down in a big book.

By this time Dash was carrying on at a great rate. He seemed to know that something important had happened to him and he ran from one side of the crate to another and poked his wet little nose through the cracks.

"Will someone please let him out?" Dot pleaded.

A strong man who was standing nearby seized one of the slats and ripped it off the crate. He picked up the dog by his collar and placed him in the arms of his new mistress.

"He's pretty heavy, isn't he?" Dot exclaimed as Dash wriggled about and nearly escaped her grasp.

Just then Mrs. Harrison came up, and she was smiling broadly.

"I am sorry I was so busy a little while ago," she said. "What did you wish to talk to me about, Dot?"

"Oh, I wanted to trade the peacock for this dog," the little girl answered. "But I don't anymore. You see, I bought Dash with my allowance so now I can have them both!"

"Well, now, that's splendid," Mrs. Harrison said heartily. "You have two pets. But I wonder what your father will say?"

Dot didn't even hear the question.

"Peacocks are pretty," she said, "but I like dogs best. Does Dash know any tricks?"

"Oh, yes, a few. You see, he is still a young dog and I have been too busy to teach him very many things. Let's take him out on the front lawn and we'll see what he can do."

The grass was tall and green on the great lawn which stretched like a rich, smooth carpet from the large white house down to the paved highway. When Mrs. Harrison set the terrier down on the soft turf he raced round and round just as fast as he could run, his ears laid back and his tail pointed straight behind.

"Oh, Mrs. Harrison!" Dot exclaimed in alarm. "Dash has gone crazy!"

"Don't be alarmed dear," Mrs. Harrison said. "He has been penned up so long that he is just celebrating a little. He will soon get tired."

Dot had never seen a dog act so in all her life. But then, she had never had a dog of her own. Those that lived on her street were pretty old and took life easy.

After awhile Dash became tired and ran slower and slower. He stopped and looked up at Mrs. Harrison as if he were expecting a little praise. His tongue was hanging out and he was panting so fast that Dot could see his ribs moving in and out.

"Why, you silly dog," she chided as she stooped to pet him. "You might have run yourself to death!"

After Dash had caught his breath again, Mrs. Harrison commanded him to sit up and speak. The terrier sat on his haunches and gave a sharp little bark.

"Oh, isn't that darling?" Dot cried as she danced up and down. "Let's see if he will do it for me."

When the little girl ordered him to sit up and speak, Dash only stood and stared at her as if he couldn't understand a single word. Then Mrs. Harrison told him to roll over. He stretched out on the grass, his four legs waving in the air. Dot commanded him to roll over too, but Dash did not obey.

"What is the matter with him, Mrs. Harrison? Why won't he do tricks for me?"

"He learned them from me and he doesn't understand when you tell him, Dot. Our voices are different and so is our way of speaking. When you get him home you can train him yourself if you are patient."

"Doesn't he know any tricks that he will do for me?"

"I think he might chase a stick or jump

through a hoop for you. He can tell what
you want him to do by your actions."

Dot found a short stick and threw it as
far as she could. Dash was after it like a
streak. He picked it up in his teeth and
laid it down at Dot's feet, looking up at her
as if to say: "Well, I hope I pleased you
that time!"

"Oh, that was fun!" Dot shouted. "Have
you a hoop, Mrs. Harrison?"

"Yes, there is one leaning against the
fence."

Dot scampered away after the hoop.
Dash thought that she wanted to run him a
race, because he reached the fence before
she did, and was waiting there when she
arrived.

Mrs. Harrison held the hoop about two
feet from the ground and said: "Jump!"
Dash sailed straight through.

"Oh, let me try it!" Dot cried.

She held the hoop just as Mrs. Harrison
had done and called out "Jump!" Dash
again leaped through the circle. Then he

gave a series of little sniffs as if he were saying something in dog language.

"What does he want, Mrs. Harrison?" Dot inquired.

"After he does his tricks, I usually give him a reward—a piece of meat is what he likes best. Dash thinks we are quite slow about it today."

"Let's give him a big bone," Dot said.

Before Mrs. Harrison could go to the kitchen after one, Doctor Davidson's car came into the farmyard, making one sharp little "honk" after another.

"Oh, there's Daddy!" Dot called excitedly. "Come on, Dash!"

Mrs. Harrison followed them to the car.

"How has Dorothy behaved?" Doctor Davidson asked, a twinkle in his eyes.

"She hasn't been a bit of trouble," the kindly lady replied.

"Just look at my new dog, Daddy!" Dot joined in, stooping down and picking up her pet. "His name is Dash and I bought him at the sale for twenty cents!"

"Twenty cents," the doctor echoed.

"Why, he looks like a pure-bred fox terrier. He is worth fifteen dollars if he is worth a penny."

"He must be worth a *hundred dollars!*" Dot declared proudly. "Why, he can roll over, sit up, speak, and jump through a hoop."

Mrs. Harrison explained how Dot had bought the dog with her own money.

"She doesn't understand the true value of the pet," the doctor said. "I can't allow her to keep it unless you'll accept an additional sum."

Mrs. Harrison replied that she really wished Dot to have the dog as a gift. The terrier had been a favorite with her and more than anything else she wanted him to have a nice home. She knew that with Dot as his mistress, he would be well treated.

"Well, I don't know what to say," Doctor Davidson hesitated. "Where do you think he could sleep after we get him home, Dot?"

"Can't he sleep with me in my room Daddy? I have a big doll bed and I could make it up for him. He would just fit.''

''I'm afraid we couldn't let him sleep in the house. It wouldn't be healthful.''

''Couldn't you give him some medicine for his germs, Daddy?'' Dot asked earnestly. ''And besides, I could give him a bath in our big white tub every day.''

The doctor and Mrs. Harrison both laughed at this but Dot couldn't see anything funny about it. She thought that it would be much better to have the bed occupied by Dash than by her dolls. Imogene, Kate, and Sarah were nice enough in their way, but they were not alive and wiggly like a little fox terrier.

''No, Dorothy,'' said her father, ''we can't let Dash sleep in our house. But we might build him a little house of his own in the back yard. How would you like that?''

''A house of his own!'' Dot repeated. She didn't quite understand.

''Yes, some call them kennels. I think Dash would be much better off if he had his own home.''

''So do I, Daddy,'' Dot agreed. ''Then

he wouldn't have to keep himself cleaned up all the time."

Doctor Davidson said that it was time for them to be getting back to Fremont. Mrs. Harrison lifted her little guest into the big car. Then she seized Dash by his collar and hoisted him in between Dot and her Daddy. She gave the terrier a final pat on the head and told him to be a good dog.

Dot waved goodbye to Mrs. Harrison and the car rolled away. Dash wriggled contentedly beside his little mistress, and she held him up so he could look out the window.

"I don't know what your mother will say when she sees us riding in with a dog," the doctor said. "Pets make a great deal of trouble."

"Dash won't make any bother," replied the little girl earnestly. "He's going to be the best dog in the world. Aren't you, Dash?"

The terrier wriggled in the arms of his young mistress and licked her hand. It was his way of saying that he would try.

CHAPTER III

A PET PEACOCK

THE automobile had traveled only a short distance when Dot suddenly sat up very straight.

"Oh, stop the car, Daddy!" she cried. "Stop the car!"

Doctor Davidson slammed on the brakes and the car halted with a lurch.

"Why, what is wrong, Dorothy?" he asked.

"Oh, Daddy," Dot said excitedly. "We're going off without my pet peacock!"

"Your peacock! Do you mean to say you've collected a peacock in addition to the dog?"

"Oh, yes, Daddy. It has the most wonderful tail in the world which spreads out like a great big fan."

"And may I ask how you acquired this

wonderful bird?" asked Doctor Davidson, his eyes twinkling.

"Mrs. Harrison gave it to me. Please, Daddy, we must turn around and go back right away."

"We can't do that, I'm afraid," replied the doctor. "I'm sure Mrs. Harrison didn't expect you to have both the peacock and the dog."

"Yes, she did, Daddy! She said so, and she's expecting us to take the peacock away."

"One pet ought to be enough, it seems to me."

"But a peacock and a dog aren't a bit alike," Dot protested. "Please, Daddy!"

Doctor Davidson frowned thoughtfully. He asked Dot to tell him exactly what Mrs. Harrison had said about the peacock. She was able to repeat the conversation almost word for word.

"I am afraid you are a little tease," her father said with a sigh. "Oh, well, we may as well have a look at the peacock."

He backed the car around in the narrow road and drove once more to the farm. Mrs. Harrison was nowhere to be seen but Dot knew the location of the peacock pen. Doctor Davidson locked Dash in the car and they walked across the yard.

"There he is, Daddy," Dot said, pointing to the peacock. "Isn't he beautiful?"

"Yes, he is a fine bird," the doctor declared admiringly. "But as a domestic pet I'm afraid he will be out of the question."

"Why, Daddy?"

Dot looked up at her father with pleading eyes.

Doctor Davidson sighed again. He knew how well the little girl liked all types of pets.

"In the first place a peacock would be a great deal of trouble," he explained. "He would eat a lot and there would be no place to keep him."

"Couldn't we give him a bed in the basement?" Dot asked hopefully. "He would be nice and warm and dry down there. And I could feed him all myself. He doesn't look hungry, does he Daddy?'' Dot asked.

When the doctor saw how his little girl had set her heart upon having the peacock, he stood in silent thought for some moments. He wanted her to have anything that would add to her knowledge, and he believed that the right kind of pets were good for a child. But a peacock was something else again.

"You're very hard to turn down, Dot," he smiled. "Are you quite sure that Mrs. Harrison wants you to have this peacock?"

"Oh, yes, Daddy!"

"Then I'll tell you what we'll do," he said. "We'll have Ben Roberts come and build him a pen out back of the garage at the same time he puts up the kennel for Dash."

"Oh, that would be wonderful, Daddy!" Dot shouted as she skipped about for sheer joy.

Ben Roberts was a nice old man who often did odd jobs about the Davidson place. It would be fun watching him build the pen. Sometimes he gave her little blocks of wood to play with, or told her stories as he pounded and sawed.

The doctor found Mrs. Harrison again, and after they had talked together, he paid her for the peacock. A stout string then was tied around the bird's legs. He was placed in a gunny-sack with only his head peeping out so he could not flay about with his strong wings.

"I hope we get home without collecting any more animals," Doctor Davidson laughed as he lifted the peacock into the back end of the coupe.

Once again the car sped along the highway. Dot wished that her father would drive still faster so that she could get home with her two wonderful new pets.

"Daddy," the little girl said after she had been silent for awhile. "I wish you would tell me a good name for my peacock."

"Well, now, that is a hard job. Let me see—"

The doctor drove along mile after mile in

a brown study but he didn't say a word.
Dot knew that he was thinking very hard.
Suddenly a name flashed into her own mind
just as if someone had whispered it to her.

"Oh, I have it, Daddy!" she cried. "Let's
call him 'Peeky'."

" 'Peeky' for peacock," her father
agreed. "Why, yes, I guess that is as good
a name as any if you like it."

In a short time they reached home and
the car rolled up the driveway. Dot saw
Mrs. Green in the back yard taking down
lace curtains from the stretchers.

"Where is Mother?" the little girl called
as she climbed out of the car holding Dash
in her arms.

"Mrs. Davidson is lyin' down," Mrs.
Green replied. "She isn't feelin' well. I
guess she shouldn't have helped me with
these curtains. It wore her out."

The laundress was so busy with her work
that she had not seen the little dog. Dot
had set Dash down on the ground. As Mrs.
Green bent over her clothes basket, the

frisky little fellow took a running leap and jumped on her with his forefeet.

Mrs. Green cried out in alarm she was so surprised, but she laughed heartily when she saw it was only a squirmy terrier.

"That pup surely gave me a fright!" she exclaimed. Then she realized that she had never seen him before and asked: "Whose dog is that?"

"Why, he's mine. His name is Dash," Dot explained. "And I have a peacock too. His name is Peeky."

"My goodness!" Mrs. Green threw up her hands in mock horror. "A peacock and a dog. What will this place become?"

"Oh, you won't have to worry, Mrs. Green," Dot said, for she saw that the laundress did not look very pleased. "Dash will have a kennel of his own and Peeky will have a pen. And I'm going to feed both of them and give them their baths."

"Whoever heard of giving a peacock a bath!" Mrs. Green laughed. "What will you think of next, Dot?"

Doctor Davidson found a long piece of rope and tied Dash to the clothes-line.

"It will only be for a day or two," he explained to Dot. "After that, Dash will know this is his home and not run away."

The peacock was more of a problem. Finally, the doctor found an old piano box in the garage which would serve for a pen until Ben Roberts could make a better one. He took a hammer and saw and fitted long strips of wood across the top of the box.

"Now Dot, you might see if you can find a vessel to hold water," he said. "Your peacock may get thirsty."

The little girl filled an empty coffee can with water and placed it in the crate. After that the Doctor untied Peeky and dropped him down into the pen.

"I'm going to tell Mother about my new pets!" Dot cried as she started toward the house.

"Don't bother her if she is sleeping," the doctor warned. "You know, Mother isn't feeling very well."

The phrase was one which Dot had heard many times during the past month. She remembered that sometimes her mother arose from the dinner table without eating a bite. Hours at a time she sat in a big easy chair by the front window, her hands lying idle in her lap. That was not like Mother.

Dot tiptoed upstairs and opened the bed-room door a tiny crack. She did not wish to awaken her mother if she were sleeping.

"Come in, dear," called a cheerful voice.

Dot went in and sat down on a footstool by the side of the bed. She thought Mother looked very pretty in her blue silk wrapper.

"Did you have a nice ride, dear?"

"Oh, yes," Dot said happily. She told Mother all about the auction sale and how she had become the owner of two unusual pets, Dash and the peacock. Mrs. Davidson said she thought a terrier would be a nice dog to have around the place.

After awhile Mrs. Green came into the room with a tray of toast and tea. She warned Dot that dinner would be served in half an hour. So the little girl kissed her mother and went to wash her face and tidy her hair.

The evening meal seemed lonesome without Mother, and Dot thought her father was quieter than usual. When dinner was over he went upstairs to the bedroom and did not return.

Dot helped Mrs. Green clear the table and wipe the dishes. She felt quite tired by that time, so she decided to put Dash to bed and then go to sleep herself.

"I'll fix up a box for the dog," Mrs. Green said kindly. "I don't want you to bother your father about it tonight, because he is worried."

They brought Dash in from outside, making up a bed for him in the furnace room. The little dog liked his new quarters. He curled up in a small round knot in his padded box and gave a satisfied sniff. In a very short time he was asleep.

The next morning Dot was happy to see her mother at the breakfast table again.

She begged her to come at once to look at the marvelous new pets. First they fed Peeky some grain, and then they carried a pan of scraps down to the little terrier.

"Isn't Dash cunning, Mother?" Dot asked proudly.

"Indeed he is," agreed Mrs. Davidson. "I think he will bring you a great deal of comfort."

After her mother had gone back upstairs, Dot sat watching Dash eat his breakfast. He seemed to be a very particular dog for he would run his nose through the food, seeking choice morsels. Best of all he liked bacon.

"And now you need some fresh air," Dot told him.

She led the terrier outside and was tying him to the clothes-line when Roger Wing skated down the Davidson driveway. At sight of Dash he did a quick turn.

"Where did you get *him*?"

"I bought him for twenty cents, only

he's worth a lot more," Dot explained. "Want to see my peacock too?"

She took him to the garage, and Roger's eyes opened wide as he peered down into the piano box.

"Peeky is nice to look at, but Dash is more fun," Dot told her little friend.

"I wish my father would buy me a dog," Roger said enviously. "Do you think he could get me one for twenty cents?"

"Mrs. Harrison doesn't have any more dogs, Roger. But I'll let you play with Dash. He can do a lot of tricks."

Dot showed him how the terrier would chase a stick.

"Most any old dog can do that," Roger said.

"Dash can jump through a hoop," Dot declared, feeling a bit hurt. "He can speak and roll over too."

The children could not find a hoop, and when Dot told Dash to roll over he did not understand.

"Oh, I guess your dog doesn't know any tricks," Roger laughed, and he skated off down the street.

Dot felt very badly then. She tried several times to make Dash sit up on his hind legs. After awhile, she grew discouraged, and tied him to the clothes-line again.

Dot saw the mailman coming down the street, so she went around to the front yard to wait for him. She was not surprised when he turned in at the Davidson's because he nearly always had letters for her father. Usually the mailman did not come until nearly noon. This morning he was early.

"I have a special delivery letter here for your mother," the mailman told Dot.

"What kind of a letter is that?" she inquired.

"It means an important letter which can't wait for the regular delivery," explained the postman. "Will you call your mother?"

Dot brought Mrs. Davidson who thanked the man and wrote her name in his little book. She glanced at the writing on the envelope.

"Why, Dot, it's from your Uncle Jack and Aunt Betty in Vermont! I wonder if anything is wrong?"

Mother looked worried as she tore open the envelope.

"Oh, please read it aloud," the little girl pleaded.

"Aunt Betty and Uncle Jack both are well," Mother laughed in relief. "The letter was sent special delivery because they want us all to come to Vermont on a visit."

She chose a paragraph from the last page and read it to Dot:

" 'Soon it will be maple sugar time in Vermont. We have been expecting a visit from you and the Doctor for a long, long time. So why not come now and help us make maple sirup at our camp? We know the quiet of the Vermont hills would do you both good, and it would be splendid for

Dorothy too. There are so many things here which would interest a child.' "

"Are we going, Mother? Are we going?"

Dot began to dance up and down she was so excited. She had seen Uncle Jack and Aunt Betty only once, but she remembered them well. They were nice and jolly and had brought her a large box of maple sugar candy.

"I wish we could go," Mother said quietly. "But I am afraid we can't make the trip just now."

"I think it would be lots of fun," Dot said hopefully.

"I don't feel able to make the trip," Mother replied. "And besides, it wouldn't be fair to Aunt Betty and Uncle Jack, for I might be taken sick while we were there."

"Daddy could give you some medicine."

"He's already given me a great deal," Mother laughed. "In fact, more than I like to take."

Dot felt disappointed about the trip, but

she did not tease. After Mother had gone
back into the house, she played with Dash
again. They were racing each other in the
yard when an old man in overalls came up
the driveway. It was Ben Roberts and he
was carrying tools.

"Oh, hello, Mr. Roberts," Dot called.
"Are you going to make a little house for
Dash and a pen for my peacock?"

"That's right," replied the workman.
"Now which shall I build first?"

"Oh, the house for Dash!"

Ben brought lumber from his car which
stood at the curbing. Dot watched him
measure off a square place on the ground,
and Dash stood right there too, as if to
oversee the job.

It was fun to watch Ben Roberts work.
First, he made a little framework, fitting it
over the place he had marked off. On the
bottom he nailed smooth floor boards and
on the roof he placed shingles like those
used for big houses. Wide, heavy boards

were nailed to the sides of the frame, so that it was all enclosed except a little door in front. It took the workman nearly all morning to make the kennel and many children from the neighborhood came in to watch him.

When it was finished at last, Dot pushed Dash in through the little door to see if he would fit.

The terrier came out in a hurry. He didn't seem to like his new home any too well.

"What is the matter with him, Mr. Roberts?" Dot asked. "Why doesn't he want to live in his new house?"

"It's all strange to him," Mr. Roberts explained. "After a few days he'll act as if he always had lived there."

In the afternoon the workman brought in more lumber and made a pen for the peacock. There was a small shed to shelter the big bird from bad weather and a place for him to strut around and spread his tail.

He wasn't frightened as Dash had been
when he was placed in his new home. Dot
thought that dogs were smarter than peacocks and more easily upset.

Ben Roberts finished his work toward the
middle of the afternoon. As he drove away,
Dot saw a nicely dressed lady who wore a
hat with a tall feather, walk up to the front
door and ring the bell.

"Why, that's Mrs. Davenport, my Sunday School teacher," Dot thought. "I want
to see *her*."

She wanted Dash to meet Mrs. Davenport too, so she wiped the mud off his paws
and let him into the house by the rear door.

Mother and the visitor had gone into the
bedroom. Mrs. Davenport took off her new
hat and laid it on the bed along with her
coat and gloves. Then they came back into
the living room.

"How do you do, Dorothy," said the
visitor. "How are you?"

"Oh, I'm just fine," Dot answered.

"And so is my new dog. I want you to meet him. Dash, this is my Sunday School teacher, Mrs. Davenport."

"I feel honored to meet you, Dash," the lady said with a smile.

She sat down by the fireplace, and the terrier came over and rubbed against her shoe. Mrs. Davenport moved slightly.

"Don't you like dogs?" Dot asked, for she saw that the lady did not seem to want Dash so near.

"Oh, yes, I like them, but I think they should stay in their proper place."

"Dash will stay in his as soon as he gets used to it," Dot told her. "You see, Ben Roberts finished his kennel only this morning."

Mother took Dash by the collar and led him away from Mrs. Davenport's chair. She told Dot that the terrier could not stay in the living room.

The little girl took her pet out into the sun room. For awhile Dash lay on the floor and allowed Dot to play with his ears.

Soon he grew restless and wandered off into another part of the house.

Mother and her guest had a long visit together, but at last Mrs. Davenport arose to leave. Dot followed them to the bedroom.

In the doorway, the two women halted in shocked surprise.

"Oh!" gasped Mrs. Davenport. "My new hat! That bad dog is ruining it!"

CHAPTER IV

DASH RUINS A HAT

DOT ran through the doorway to see what had happened.

There on the bed was Dash! In his mouth the mischievous little dog held Mrs. Davenport's new hat. He shook it and growled.

"Oh, Dash, what have you done?" cried Mrs. Davidson. "Drop it!"

Dot ran forward and seized the terrier by the collar. He would not let go of the hat. Instead, he stiffened his legs and threw his weight backward in quick little jumps. He nearly jerked away from her.

Then Dot snatched him up in her arms and gave him a hard shake. Dash was so surprised that he dropped the hat. Mrs. Davidson quickly picked it up.

"Oh, it's ruined," she said in distress. The crown of the hat had lost all shape and the feather was in tatters. Dash had done a thorough job.

"I can't tell you how sorry I am," Mother said to her guest. "Of course I shall buy you a new hat."

Dot felt very badly about it too. She had hoped that Dash would prove himself a model dog and he had disgraced himself on the second day she owned him.

"You bad dog," she scolded as she carried him in disgrace to his kennel. "Aren't you ashamed to ruin a nice hat?"

Dash seemed to know that he had disappointed his little mistress. His tail drooped and he looked up at her as if asking forgiveness.

"You must stay here until you've decided to be a good dog," Dot told him.

She fasted his chain so that he could not run away. By the time she returned to the house, Mrs. Davenport had gone. Dot asked if the lady had left without taking her hat.

"I loaned her one of mine," Mrs. David-

son said. "Oh, I was never so humiliated
in my life."

"Dash didn't mean to do wrong, Mother."

"I'm sure he didn't, dear, but after this
we must watch him more closely. I can't
allow him in the house at all if he misbe-
haves."

The next two or three days, Dash proved
himself to be a model dog. Dot spent
nearly all of her waking hours with him
out of doors. Several times her father had
to remind her to feed the peacock but she
never forgot about Dash's food.

Roger liked to play with Dash too and he
tried to make him sit up and shake hands.
The little dog would jump through a hoop
and bring back a stick, but that was all.

"I wonder why he is so stubborn with us?"
Dot asked. "He would do so many things
for Mrs. Harrison."

"I think he'd sit up if we had a piece of
meat to feed him."

"I'll get some from Mrs. Green!" Dot
cried.

She ran into the house but the laundress was not in the kitchen. Dot could hear her moving about upstairs. She didn't want to call her, for she knew that Mother was trying to sleep again.

Dot opened the refrigerator door. On the lower shelf was a nice raw roast wrapped up in paper. The piece was much too large to give Dash, but Dot didn't know how to cut off a small chunk for she had been told never to touch the sharp knives in the kitchen drawer.

The little girl was trying to twist off a small corner when Mrs. Green came down the stairway.

"Dorothy Davidson!" she exclaimed. "What are you doing with that roast?"

"I was going to give some of it to Dash. He always likes a piece of meat when he does a trick."

Mrs. Green slammed shut the refrigerator door.

"I may do a few tricks of my own if I catch you feeding my good roast to Dash," she said crossly. Then seeing Dot's hurt little face, she added more kindly: "There, I know you didn't stop to think. I'll give you a nice piece of bacon."

"Dash is very fond of bacon," Dot said, brightening.

She carried the meat out to the back yard. Dash smelled it right away and came running to her.

"Hold up the piece of bacon," Roger told her. "Sit up, Dash! Sit up!"

At first the little dog would not obey, but when he saw that Dot would not let him have the meat unless he did, he sat on his haunches and begged.

"Oh, isn't that cute!" Dot cried in delight. "Here, Dash, you may have your reward."

The terrier gulped down the meat and stood looking at her greedily. The bacon was all gone and he would not do the trick without it.

After awhile the children grew tired of playing with Dash. They put him back in his kennel but the terrier would not stay there.

"I don't see what is the matter with him," said Dot. "Here he has a nice home and he doesn't like it."

"Maybe the floor is too hard," Roger told her. "Dash ought to have a nice soft bed."

"Let's look in the garage for a gunny sack," Dot suggested.

The children searched everywhere but they could not find anything which would serve as a pad for Dash's kennel.

"Mrs. Green has a lot of old rags in the basement," Dot said. "Maybe I can find something there."

The little girl ran into the house, calling the housekeeper's name. Mrs. Green did not answer for she was upstairs again.

Dot ran down the basement stairs intending to look in the rag bag which hung by the furnace. As she passed through the laundry room she saw an old, tattered coverlet hanging on the line. It was made of heavy wool and had little pine-tree figures along the border.

"That would be just the thing for Dash's bed!" Dot thought.

The little girl was quite sure that Mother never used the coverlet. The fringe was badly frayed and there were several holes in the soft wool.

Dot pulled the coverlet down from the line and carried it back to the kennel. She and Roger folded it into a small square so that it was an exact fit for the floor of Dash's home.

"There! He does like it!" Roger cried gaily as the terrier snuggled down into the warm bed.

It was growing late in the afternoon. Mrs. Wing came down the street to tell Roger that he must come home. Dot felt lonesome without her little playmate. Her fingers were beginning to tingle with cold, so she went indoors to warm them.

Mrs. Green helped Dot take off her heavy coat and mittens. Usually the housekeeper laughed and talked with the little girl, but this time she scarcely spoke a word. She seemed worried about something.

"Is anything wrong, Mrs. Green?" Dot asked.

Mrs. Green gave her a tiny hug. "Nothing that you're to fret about, honey."

Dot turned toward the stairway. She wanted to tell Mother about how Dash had decided to like his new kennel.

"No, dear, don't go up there now," Mrs. Green said quickly. "Your father is with Mrs. Davidson."

"Why I didn't hear Daddy come home!"

"I sent for him in a hurry," Mrs. Green told her gravely. "Your mother is having another one of her hard pains."

"Is she lots worse?" Dot asked anxiously.

"I'm afraid she is, dear. But don't you worry. One of these days she'll go off to the city and when she comes back she'll be well again."

Mrs. Green took Dot by the hand and led her to the kitchen.

"How would you like to help me make cookies?" she asked brightly. "Wouldn't that be fun?"

"I'll make some for Mother," Dot said. "Will she be able to eat them, Mrs. Green?"

"I think she might," the housekeeper nodded.

Dot carefully washed her hands and put on an apron. Then Mrs. Green mixed a cookie batter in a large blue bowl. She gave Dot some of the dough to roll out with her own tiny rolling pin.

It took the little girl a long while to cut the cookies into fancy shapes. Long before she had a pan of them ready to bake, Mrs. Green had whisked all of hers into the oven.

"Now while they're baking I'll run downstairs and get the coverlet I washed this morning," said the housekeeper. "It should be dry by now."

In a few minutes Mrs. Green came back looking very disturbed.

"Someone has taken your mother's coverlet off the line," she told Dot. "The gas

meter man was here today, but I can't believe he'd take it."

"Do you mean that old ragged blanket
with the pine trees?" Dot asked.

"Old ragged blanket!" Mrs. Green exclaimed. "Why, that coverlet has been in
this family for more than seventy years. It
is one of your mother's most choice posses-
sions."

"I thought it was just an old blanket,"
Dot said. "That's why I gave it to Dash for
a bed."

"You gave that coverlet to your dog!
Dorothy Davidson—"

"But Mrs. Green, he needed something
soft and warm," Dot told her. "I didn't
know Mother ever used it."

"There, child, it's all right," Mrs. Green
said in a more gentle tone. "Run right out
now and get the coverlet. I'll have to wash
it again."

Dot did not like to take the coverlet away
from Dash. The terrier had snuggled down
into its soft woolen folds and he looked of-

fended when she pulled it from beneath him.
He stood up and barked his protest.

"Don't you worry, Dash," the little girl
whispered to comfort him. "I'll find you
something else."

When Dot went back into the house with
the coverlet, Mrs. Green was taking a pan of
cookies from the oven.

"I guess no harm has been done," she said,
carefully examining the blanket. "I'll find
something else for Dash."

Dot was looking hard at the pan of cookies.

"Please, could I have just one?" she
pleaded.

Mrs. Green started to say that it would
spoil Dot's dinner, but just then she heard
Doctor Davidson coming down the stairway.

"Yes, you may have just one," she said
hurriedly and went into the other room to
speak with the doctor.

While Dot ate her cookie she could hear
Mrs. Green and her father talking very
earnestly. After awhile the housekeeper
came back to the kitchen.

"I'll finish baking the cookies, Dot," she said kindly. "Your father wishes to talk with you."

The little girl walked slowly into the living room. She was afraid she might be scolded about the coverlet, but Doctor Davidson did not look stern as he lifted her on his knee.

"Dorothy," he said, "how would you like to spend a few weeks in Vermont?"

Dot drew in her breath. A vacation with Uncle Jack and Aunt Betty! How splendid that would be.

"Oh, Daddy," she cried in delight, "when are we going? When are we going, Daddy?"

CHAPTER V

ABOARD THE TRAIN

"YOUR mother and I won't be able to make the trip," Doctor Davidson explained. "At least we'll go only part of the way. But you'd not be afraid to ride on the train alone."

"Oh, no, Daddy!" Dot declared.

"Your uncle and aunt want you with them in Vermont," the doctor went on quietly. "It seems best to send you there."

"Maybe Uncle Jack will let me help him make maple sugar," Dot laughed. "That would be fun. Only it would be lots nicer if you and Mother went too."

Doctor Davidson gave her a tender squeeze. "We don't want to send you off alone, Dot, but there's no other way. You see, I am taking Mother to a big hospital in New York."

"And when she comes back home she'll be well again?"

"Yes, Dot, I'm sure it will be that way."

"Maybe I could go with you, Daddy."

"I'm afraid not," her father said slowly. "We can't leave you here either, for the house will be closed. Mrs. Green will be away visiting a relative."

Dot was silent for a moment. Then she asked anxiously:

"May I take Dash with me to Vermont?"

"Why, I imagine your Aunt Betty wouldn't mind. Dash might keep you from being so lonesome."

"And Peeky?"

"You couldn't very well take him to Vermont. I'm afraid we'll have to give the peacock away."

"Give Peeky away!" Dot cried in an outraged little voice. "Oh, Daddy! You wouldn't do that!" I'd rather stay home from Vermont than lose my peacock."

"I thought you were growing tired of

him," the doctor said hastily. "We'll try to find someone who will feed him while we're gone."

"Roger would do it, Daddy. He likes Peeky and would give him enough to eat."

"We'll see," promised the doctor. "I'm sure everything will work out."

Dot had little time the next two days to think about the peacock, because Mrs. Green took her down town to buy new clothes for the trip. There were suitcases to pack, Imogene's wardrobe to prepare and many little friends one must bid farewell.

Roger felt very downhearted because Dot was leaving.

"I wish I could go too," he said wistfully. "You'll have fun in the mountains."

"I'll send you some of Uncle Jack's maple sugar," Dot promised, trying to cheer him up. "And you'll earn a whole dollar!"

Doctor Davidson had told Roger he would give him this sum for looking after the peacock. Dot knew that sometimes the little boy forgot to do things, but Mrs. Wing had said she would help take care of Peeky.

"I wish you'd leave Dash here," Roger said, brightening. "I wouldn't charge anything to look after *him*."

"I'd never go away without Dash," Dot declared loyally.

The next morning Mrs. Green awoke the little girl almost before it was daylight to dress her for the train trip. Dot was so excited she couldn't stand still while the housekeeper combed her hair.

Mother sat quietly in a chair watching Doctor Davidson strap the luggage. She kept looking about the room as if she hated the thought of leaving it.

"How fast time is slipping away," she said.

"Now don't you worry," Mrs. Green told her cheerfully. "Everything will come out right, I know. You'll return home well and strong."

"Of course I shall," replied Mother with

a smile. She drew Dot to her chair and gave her a loving squeeze.

Soon a taxi cab came to the door and the driver carried out their luggage. Dot held Dash in her arms, and when Mrs. Green kissed her goodbye, she had to hug both the little girl and her dog.

"Goodbye, Mrs. Green," Dot called as the car rolled away. "Don't forget to write."

They sped past the Wing house, and she waved again at Roger who was watching from his front porch. The cab came at last to the railroad station.

"Let me lead Dash," Dot said as her father lifted her to the ground. "I think he's a little worried about riding on the train."

Doctor Davidson placed the leash in her hand and then helped Mother from the cab. "First we'll get the tickets," he said, "and then we'll take Dash to the baggage room."

"The baggage room!" Dot repeated. "Isn't Dash going to ride with us?"

"Dogs are not allowed in the Pullman

cars," her father explained. "Dash will
have to ride with the trunks and suit-cases."

"Do we have to put him in a trunk?" Dot
asked, very much worried.

"Oh, no. He will be tied by his leash so he
can't get away. The baggageman will take
good care of him."

"But Daddy," said Dot, for she did not
understand it at all. "How will Dash know
when it's time for him to get off the train?"

"I will check him right through to Mapletown. When you reach there, Dash will be
in the baggage car waiting for you."

Dot felt better then. She knew her Daddy
would arrange things so that Dash would be
all right. But she could not help feeling a
little disappointed. She had hoped to have
Dash ride with her on the train. There would
be so many new and interesting things for
him to watch from the window.

In the baggage room of the station, Dash
seemed to feel very much at home. He was
not frightened by the big trucks piled high
with luggage which rolled by. It was all

very exciting to him and he tugged so hard on his leash that Dot had to lean back on her heels to hold him.

"Is this the dog for Mapletown?" asked the baggageman, smiling at Dot. He wore a blue uniform and a cap with a shiny badge.

"Yes, we're checking him straight through," replied Doctor Davidson. "Dot, give the man your leash. He will take charge of Dash."

Dot did not want to say goodbye to her dog but there was no other way. She stooped down and gave him a final pat on the head.

"Everything will be all right, Dash," she said. "Don't you worry."

The baggageman led the dog away. Dot then followed her parents to the crowded waiting room of the station. Doctor Davidson paced up and down and compared his watch with the big clock on the wall.

Soon Dot heard a man call out at the top of his voice:

"Number sixteen. For Buff-a-lo, Sy-racuse, Al-bany and New York. Train on track two.''

''Who is that man, Mother?'' Dot asked. ''What makes him talk so loud?''

''He is the train caller, dear. He speaks loudly so the people will be sure to hear and not miss their train.''

''He called our train,'' the doctor added. ''Come along, Dot.''

She clung tightly to his hand as they mingled with the crowd. They went through a large iron gate where a man in uniform looked at their tickets. A porter took their hand luggage and saw them settled in their comfortable Pullman seats.

''I wish we were going all the way to Vermont with Dorothy,'' Mrs. Davidson said as the train began to move. ''I don't like to send her on alone from the junction.''

''Dot will be in good hands,'' the doctor replied. ''And the experience should broaden her. Travel has that effect.''

Dot thought about the remark as she

played with Imogene. She kept wriggling about in the seat, and looking down at the sash of her dress.

"Oh, Mother," she said at last, "how long will I have to travel before I get wider?"

"I surely don't know what you mean," laughed Mrs. Davidson. "You will become larger as you grow older, of course."

"But Daddy said travel would broaden me."

Mrs. Davidson put her handkerchief to her mouth and quickly looked out the Pullman window. The doctor lowered his newspaper and laughed aloud.

"Your father didn't mean that your body would become broader," Mother explained kindly. "He was talking about your mind. When one has new experiences and sees new things, one learns a great deal. That is what Daddy meant by saying that travel is broadening."

The train rushed along through towns and cities, over high bridges and past tall forests. Dot listened to the click of the rails until the sound made her drowsy. When she awoke her father was shaking her gently.

"Time to wake up, Dorothy."

"Are we in Vermont, Daddy?" she asked.

"No, only the Junction. This train goes on. You must wait here and take another which will carry you to Uncle Jack and Aunt Betty."

Mother bundled Dot into her coat and hat. Then the doctor carried her suitcase while Mother led her by the hand out of the train and into the station.

"We have only a minute to say goodbye, dear," Mother said, and there were tears in her eyes. "The station matron will take care of you and see that you are put on your train."

"Uncle Jack and Aunt Betty will meet you at Mapletown," the doctor added. "You have money in your purse if you wish to buy anything on the train. The conductor will be told to look after you."

"Be a brave little girl," said Mother tenderly, for she saw that Dot was about to cry. "Daddy will write you a long letter when we get to New York."

The little girl kissed her parents goodbye. She tried hard not to cry but a stray tear trickled down her cheek. Then the matron took her by the hand and led her away. "Your train doesn't leave for half an hour," the woman told her kindly. "We'll find a picture book for you to look at while you wait."

Dot didn't care about looking at pictures but she was too polite to say so. She felt very much alone in the world. Dash was somewhere in a baggage car, and her mother and father were speeding on to New York. She couldn't help feeling lonesome and blue even though the gray-haired station matron was very kind.

Dot was quite worried about Dash. She wondered if he had been put off at the junction and if he would catch his train too when it came. Anxiously, she asked the matron what became of dogs that missed their trains.

"Oh, that seldom happens," the woman answered, "but when it does, they are sent along on the next one."

Dot thought that time passed very slowly. She would look at the picture book for a little while and then gaze at the clock. The hands did not appear to move at all.

"Your train is here, Dorothy," said the station matron at last.

A colored porter came to carry Dot's traveling bag. Then the matron went with the little girl out to the train and placed her in the care of the Pullman conductor. She gave him the ticket, but she handed Dot a little piece of white printed paper, warning her to keep it safe. It was the claim check for Dash.

"When you get to Mapletown," said the matron, "just give this to the station agent. Then he'll let you have your dog. You'll be careful not to lose the check?"

"Oh, yes," promised Dot, "I'll be real careful."

She placed the card in her little purse

along with the money which her father had given her. Then Dot thanked the matron and waved goodbye to her as she walked away from the station platform.

There was a clanking sound and the hiss of air from the brakes. Slowly the train started to move. Dot looked out the window again and saw group after group of people waving goodbye to their friends who were on the train.

"Vermont must be a wonderful place," the little girl thought. "So many folks are going there."

It was after twelve o'clock and Dot was very hungry. Her Daddy had told her to call the colored porter or the conductor whenever she was ready to have her dinner. She found a tiny button near the window and timidly pressed it. Her father had explained that it would ring a bell in another part of the car.

The negro porter came down the aisle, smiling at the little girl. She looked up at him very timidly, her mouth trembling.

and a tall glass of milk.   For dessert Dot had
a large dish of chocolate ice cream.

"Oh, dear, I feel stuffed!" she said to
herself as she looked at the empty dishes.
"I hope I don't get sick."

The waiter brought a bill and laid it down
by her plate.

"How much does it say, Mister Waiter?"
Dot asked.

"One dollar and ten cents."

Dot opened her purse and gave the man
two dollars.

He took the money and soon returned with
ninety cents in silver on a little tray.   Dot
collected the coins and put them back in her
purse.

The dining car steward came and asked
the little girl if she had enjoyed her dinner.

"Oh, yes, very much," she replied.   "You
serve 'specially nice ice cream."

A waiter then took Dot back to her Pullman seat and the porter brought her a large,
white pillow for her head.

"Dat's my treat to you, Miss!" he explained. "You is gettin' twenty-five cents worth o' free pillow."

Dot thanked the porter and snuggled down in the cushions. After awhile she noticed that Imogene had slumped down in a corner of the seat. She picked her up to straighten her crumpled dress and smooth her hair. Imogene wasn't standing the trip nearly as well as her young mother.

"There, Imogene, you sit by the window," she said soothingly. "A little fresh air will do you good."

Dot rested her head against the pillow again but she could not go to sleep. She kept thinking about Dash and wondering if he were lonesome. She hoped the baggage man had not forgotten to give him his dinner.

Dot dug down into her little purse to see if the claim check was still safe. She gave a startled cry. It was not there! Even when she emptied everything from the purse she could not find it. She had lost Dash's claim check.

In a panic, Dot called the colored porter who was passing down the aisle.

"Oh, Mr. Porter," she said, almost in tears. "I have lost the claim check for my dog. Now they will never give him back to me."

"Don't you worry," he said. "Tell me, where you been keepin' it."

"Right here in my purse, and it's gone."

"Now think hard, Miss. Where 'bouts you open it up last?"

At first Dot could not remember. Then she knew it was in the dining car when she had paid for her dinner.

"You all stay right heah, Miss," the porter told her. "I'll go up dere and do some fancy lookin'."

It seemed to Dot that he was gone a long, long while. But the porter was grinning broadly as he came down the aisle and he held something in his hand.

"Heah's yo' dog ticket," he said, giving her the claim check. "It was layin' right undeh yo' table."

Dot thanked the porter for his kindness and put Dash's check in her purse again. This time she would be careful and not let it drop out.

After so much excitement and worry the little girl felt very tired. She dropped her head down on the big pillow and soon was sleeping soundly. She was awakened by a gentle tug at her arm.

"Mapletown is de next stop," the porter was saying. "Yo' betteh rouse yo' self."

Dot barely had time to get Imogene back into her traveling bag, before the train stopped at the Mapletown station. The porter carried her luggage and helped her alight from the car. Dot told him goodbye and then gazed anxiously about.

She saw a well-built, tall man and a plump lady with gray hair coming toward her. They were both smiling broadly.

"Oh, hello, Uncle Jack and Aunt Betty!" Dot cried.

"Welcome to Vermont!" laughed Uncle Jack as he reached down to pick up her suitcase. "Better button up that coat. It's cold here in the mountains."

"Did you have a nice trip?" asked Aunt Betty after she had given Dot a kiss.

"Oh, yes, but I'm worried about Dash. He's in the baggage car, and they may forget to take him out."

"We'll get Dash all right," laughed Uncle Jack. "Do you have a claim check?"

Dot had not lost the ticket a second time. She took it from her purse and gave it to her uncle. The train pulled out of the station.

"Where is Dash?" the little girl asked.

"That's what I wonder myself," answered Uncle Jack. "But probably he's been taken inside the station."

They went into the building. It was several minutes before the baggage man came to wait on them. Uncle Jack gave him the check.

Dot could tell by the way the man looked that something was wrong.

"A dog?" he asked in surprise. "Sorry, but there's no dog here."

CHAPTER VI

A MISSING DOG

UPON hearing the baggage man's words, Dot jerked free from Uncle Jack and ran to the door of the station. She felt certain that Dash had been carried on past Mapletown. But she could never stop the train now. It was far down the track.

"Oh, I just knew something would happen to Dash," she wailed. "They forgot to take him out of the car."

"There was no dog on this train," said the baggage man, "so he couldn't have been carried past. Probably he'll come along on the next train."

"And when is that?" asked Uncle Jack.

"At five twenty-eight. I take it you're in a hurry to get back to The Maples?"

"Well, yes, we are," said Uncle Jack, frowning. "There's chores to be done."

"We'll take good care of the dog when he

86

comes in," promised the baggage man. "You could pick him up the next time you're in town."

Uncle Jack glanced at Dot and shook his head.

"No, that would never do. The little girl needs her dog right away. We'll loaf around town until the next train comes in."

Dot wished to wait right in the station, but Aunt Betty told her that would not be necessary. It was several hours before the train was due and they would have time to do a little shopping and go to a moving picture show.

First they went to a grocery store where Uncle Jack bought several large boxes of food which were carried out to his car.

"Our maple sugar camp is way up in the hills," Uncle Jack explained to Dot. "It's hard to get to town more than once a week, so we buy enough to last.

It was easy for the little girl to talk with her uncle and aunt. She felt as if she had known them always. She answered all their questions about her mother and father, and told them about Roger, and how he was taking care of the peacock.

Then they went to a picture show, and if Dot hadn't been so worried about Dash she would have enjoyed every minute of it.

"It's after five o'clock," said Uncle Jack.

The afternoon had passed very swiftly and now it was time for them to go back to the station after Dash.

Dot did not have long to wait. Soon the big train came puffing into the station. Uncle Jack and Aunt Betty took her by the hand, and they walked down the platform to watch the baggage car being unloaded. The little girl held her breath. If Dash hadn't been sent on this train—

But there he was! She gave a cry of joy as she saw the baggage man lift him out of the car.

"Oh, Dash, you little darling!" she laughed as she ran to him. The station agent gave her his leash.

Dash seemed just as glad to see Dot as she

was to see him. He barked and capered about her. As she held out her hand to him he would leap into the air and try to caress it.

"Oh, Dash, you're so excited," Dot chided as she stooped to pet him. "But I don't wonder for you've had a long ride."

"He looks like a very fine dog," said Aunt Betty.

"Dash is the finest dog in the world," Dot told her proudly. "He can do a lot of tricks only he won't do all of them for me. Won't you sit up and speak?"

The little girl did not expect Dash to obey. She was very much surprised when he slowly raised up, waving his forepaws and looking at his mistress proudly.

"Why, he'll do it for me now!" Dot shouted in delight. "Roll over, Dash! Roll over!"

Dash did not disappoint her. He rolled over just as if it were a very ordinary thing to do.

"He understands what I say to him now!"

Dot cried. She caught Dash up in her arms and gave him a hug. "Oh, I guess you're just so glad to see me that you're willing to obey!"

"I don't like to break up this happy reunion," laughed Uncle Jack, "but it will soon be dark. We ought to be starting for the camp."

"Is it very far?" asked Dot.

"No, only about five miles from town," Aunt Betty replied. "But the road is steep."

Dot led Dash to the car and snuggled beside him in the back seat. Aunt Betty sat with her, wrapping a warm blanket over their knees.

"We're starting up Bread Loaf mountain now," Uncle Jack called from the front seat as the car left the road. "It's really only a steep hill."

"They call it Bread Loaf because from a distance the peak is rounded over like a loaf of bread," Aunt Betty explained.

For a few minutes it seemed to Dot that they drove straight up into the sky. The

road twisted and turned and was so steep
that the engine groaned and puffed.

"The worst of the climb is behind us now,"
said Uncle Jack.

They passed through an old covered bridge
and for a little way followed the bed of a
swift-moving stream. It gurgled and
splashed against the white rocks, churning
up great mounds of foam.

"Oh, see the pretty waterfall!" Dot cried
as the car turned a sharp bend.

"That is only a tiny one," said Aunt Betty.
"We will pass more interesting ones before
we reach our camp."

The car gave a sudden skid on the road
and nearly went into the ditch. Uncle Jack
turned the steering wheel just in time to
prevent an accident.

"Oh, Jack, do be careful!" Aunt Betty
warned anxiously. "It's getting colder and
the roads are starting to freeze again."

"Yes, we'll have to go slower," Uncle Jack
agreed. "This highway has a gravel base,
but during the day the warm sun melts the

snow. Then as evening comes on it freezes.''

"At that we shouldn't complain,'' said Aunt Betty, "for it's perfect weather for sugaring.''

Dot was glad when her aunt explained what she meant by 'sugaring weather.' During the daytime sap started to run in the trunks of the maple trees, but at night it was just cold enough to freeze it again.

"All of the farmers are tapping their maples now,'' Aunt Betty declared. "Our camp has been running for several days.''

"May I help make maple sugar?'' Dot asked eagerly.

"We'll start you to work early tomorrow morning,'' Uncle Jack said heartily. "That is, if you can get up.''

"Oh, I'll be awake early,'' Dot laughed.

"I'll bet you can't even tell a maple tree from a pine,'' teased Uncle Jack.

"Oh, yes, I can,'' Dot replied proudly. "We have a maple tree in our yard at home. In the spring it has little seeds on it that will squirt when you pinch them!''

"That's right," laughed Uncle Jack. "Only your tree is probably a soft maple. The ones in Vermont are hard maples and their sap is better for maple sirup and sugar."

"You'll learn all about it tomorrow when you see the men at work," Aunt Betty promised.

After awhile the car turned into a still narrower road.

"We're coming to our place now," Uncle Jack said. "The sugar camp is over to the right, but it's hidden by the trees. The house is just over the brow of this knoll."

It had grown so dark that Dot could not see very well. A minute later the car turned into a barnyard, and then she caught a glimpse of a faded old white house. It looked very gloomy in the shadows.

"Well, here we are," laughed Uncle Jack, lifting her down.

"Is it all right for Dash to come into the house too?" Dot asked as Aunt Betty opened the gate for her.

"Sure thing," chuckled Uncle Jack. "We couldn't let him stay outdoors these cold nights. He'd freeze his paws."

Aunt Betty opened the door of the house and lighted a lamp. While she helped Dot off with her coat, Uncle Jack threw a shovel of coal into the kitchen stove. Soon the room was cozy and warm.

"It won't take me a minute to get supper," said Aunt Betty. "You must be very hungry, Dot."

The little girl helped set the table in the kitchen and very soon everything was ready. They had sausage cakes with mashed potatoes and thick, cream gravy, carrots, and large wedges of custard pie. And as an extra treat, Dot found a tiny square of maple sugar at her plate.

"Oh, it's good!" she declared. "May Dash have a little piece too?"

"Yes," laughed Aunt Betty, "but I think a juicy bone would be much better for him. I'll have to watch both of you while you're here to see that you don't eat too much maple sugar."

"I could never have enough," said Dot greedily.

The little girl was so tired that Aunt Betty said she need not help with the dishes. First, Dash was given a snug bed by the woodbox, and then Dot was tucked under the covers in a bedroom over the kitchen.

"Sleep tight," said Aunt Betty as she bade her good night. "You must rest well so that you'll be ready to go sugaring in the morning."

"Don't forget to wake me early," pleaded Dot, and she snuggled down under the warm blankets and went off to sleep.

CHAPTER VII

MAKING MAPLE SUGAR

IT was cold in the bedroom when Dot woke
up the next morning. The little girl felt the
icy air bite her skin as she sprang from beneath the covers. She began to pull on her
clothes as fast as she could.

"Bring your shoes down to the kitchen,"
Aunt Betty told her. "It's nice and warm
there."

The kitchen was fragrant with the odor of
coffee and frying bacon. While Aunt Betty
flipped pancakes, Dash sat close by the stove,
watching her. Now and then he gave a little
bark. He expected her to miss the pan with
one of her cakes, but she never did.

Breakfast was soon ready. Dot felt
ashamed at the number of pancakes she ate,
but Aunt Betty didn't seem to think it was
too many.

"Don't be afraid to eat heartily," she

urged the little girl. "You'll be hungry before noon."

Uncle Jack had put on his heavy coat and
galoshes. He took a little pair of boots from
the kitchen closet.

"The snow is still deep up where we're
going," he told Dot. "You'll need these to
keep your feet warm and dry."

He helped her draw on the boots, while
Aunt Betty brought mittens and a thick wool
scarf.

"Now you wait here until I hitch up the
team," Uncle Jack directed. "It won't take
me long."

He went out to the barn. Dot watched
from the window. When she saw that the
horses were hitched up to the bob-sled, she
and Dash ran out.

"Up you go," laughed Uncle Jack, and he
lifted them both into the sled.

The road was bare of snow in many places,
but when they cut through the pasture the
sled ran better.

"You can see the sugar house from here,"

said Uncle Jack. He pointed to a log building directly ahead. Blue smoke was curling
up from its chimney.

"Is someone there already?" asked Dot.

"Oh, yes, Jeff—he's my hired man—has
been at work for a couple of hours. Most
likely he has some sirup made by this time."

Uncle Jack stopped the team which stood
without hitching. He helped Dot down and
Dash leaped out into a snow bank.

"We'll take a look inside the sugar house
before we start gathering sap," Uncle Jack
said.

He flung open the door of the cabin and
called out a greeting to Jeff. For a minute
Dot could not see anything except smoke and
steam. Then she made out her uncle's
helper, a boy of sixteen, who was throwing
wood on the fire under the boiler.

"Hello, Jeff, I've brought you a couple of
visitors," said Uncle Jack. "Meet Dot and
Dash. They want to learn how maple sugar
is made."

"I'll soon be sugarin' off," replied Jeff

with a grin. "The sirup is just about ready."

Dot had a great many questions to ask. First she wanted to know about the huge square boiler which nearly filled the sugar house. The top was covered with a shallow pan divided into units. Each compartment was filled with a liquid, but only the third section seemed to contain pure, golden sirup.

"It's like this," explained Uncle Jack. "You see that pipe leading into the boiler? Well, it connects with a large vat outside the shack which we keep filling with sap from the maple trees. It runs into this first section of pans on the stove. After it boils there for a while, it passes into the next section. There it thickens and finally runs into the third pan where it stays until it is ready to draw off into cans."

"And then is it sirup?" Dot asked.

"Yes, you had some just like it for breakfast this morning."

"How do you make maple sugar, Uncle Jack?"

"No, we'll use only a very small part of it," explained Uncle Jack. "We'll not hurt the tree in the least."

As Dot walked beside her uncle, she thought of another question. She inquired if only maple trees had sap.

"All trees have it, and so have plants," answered Uncle Jack. "But only the hard maple sap is suitable for sirup and sugar."

Dot and her uncle went from tree to tree emptying the pails of sap into a larger bucket.

"May I have a drink, Uncle Jack?"

"Take as much as you want, Dot."

She took a bucket from one of the trees and tipped it up so that she could drink. The sap was icy cold but Dot liked the sweetish flavor. When she replaced the empty pail on the metal spout, the sap dripped into it again, "ting, ting, ting," so fast that it almost ran in a stream.

Uncle Jack carried his large bucket back to the sled and emptied it into a huge wooden hogshead. He made the trip several times until the container would hold no more.

"Now we'll go back to the sugar house," Uncle Jack declared.

"Here, Dash," called Dot, for the terrier had scampered off through the woods.

Uncle Jack clucked to the horses and they trotted down the road. When the sled went over a bump sap splashed out the top of the hogshead. Only a very little was lost for the center hole was not large.

At the sugar house, Uncle Jack fastened a spigot to the bottom of the hogshead. Then he let the sap run off into the large vat.

"Now I must go back again," said Uncle Jack. "Will you stay here with Jeff or go with me?"

"I'll stay," Dot decided. Her fingers were beginning to tingle and she wanted to warm them by the fire.

Jeff was working by the big iron kettle when the little girl went inside.

"You're just in time to see me make sugar," he told her. "The sirup is starting to grain now."

While Dot warmed her hands by the fire, she watched the boy work. He stirred and stirred the liquid in the kettle and she could see it getting thicker and thicker, almost like mush.

"Now it's ready to pour into the tubs," said Jeff. "Step back because I must work fast, and some of the hot sugar might splash."

Dot moved out of the way. After Jeff had filled the tubs, he poured a little of the thick sirup into smaller molds.

"Could I have one of those?" the little girl asked.

"Just as soon as it's cold," promised Jeff. "Here, while you're waiting I'll show you how to make some sugar of your own."

He took a tin dipper and scooped the last of the sirup out of the kettle.

"We'll have to find some clean snow now," he said.

They discovered a nice untrampled snow bank close to the shack. Jeff patted down a smooth place with his mittens. Then he poured some of the hot sirup over it in the form of writing, spelling out the word, "Dot!"

"Now when it cools you can eat your own name," Jeff laughed.

"Oh, let me try it!" Dot pleaded. "Let me make some snow sugar!"

Jeff gave her the pan and went back into the shack.

"I'll make some maple sugar for you, Dash," the little girl told her dog.

She wrote his name in the hard-packed snow, only the letters weren't very easy to read. She ran out of sirup before she finished the last one which was "h".

By that time the first snow sugar had cooled. It was hard and waxy, not like the cake sugar, but even though it wasn't easy to eat, Dot found it very good. She ate Dash's share too because he didn't seem to want it.

When Dot went back into the sugar house, Jeff was pouring maple sirup into shiny square cans.

"Are the little cakes hard yet?" asked Dot.

"Yes, here is one for you." Jeff took it out of the mold and gave it to her.

By the time she had finished eating it, Uncle Jack came back with another hogshead of sap. After he had poured it into the vat he stepped into the shack to see how Dot was getting along.

"We'll have to send your mother and father a box of sugar," he told Dot. "Would you like to do that?"

"Oh, yes!" Dot cried eagerly. Then she became sober. "But I don't know where my Mother and Daddy are now."

"It takes a long while for a letter to get to Mapletown," replied Uncle Jack. "You'll probably hear from your folks tomorrow. But anyhow, Aunt Betty has their address."

"I'd like to send them a big box of maple sugar, Uncle Jack. And one to Mrs. Green! And Roger!"

"Well, well, that's a large order," laughed Uncle Jack. "But we have plenty of sugar

this year, so I think we can handle it. Would
you like to pack the boxes yourself?"

Dot said that she would, so her uncle gave
her three small containers which had been
made especially to hold maple sugar. She
selected the nicest cakes and stacked them
neatly in the boxes.

Little crumbs kept breaking off from some
of the pieces of sugar, and Dot ate them all.

When she had finished packing the boxes,
one cake was left.

"May I have it, Uncle Jack?" she asked.

"Why, I guess so," he answered. "How
many have you had?"

"Only one cake that Jeff gave me," Dot
replied. She did not think to tell him about
the sugar snow or all the crumbs she had
eaten.

Uncle Jack kept making trips in his sled
to gather sap. Sometimes he took Dot and
Dash with him, but usually they stayed at
the shack with Jeff.

There were a number of large maple trees
close by, and the little girl liked to watch

the buckets fill. Then she would carry them to the vat and empty them herself. She kept noticing the sirup boiler too, and when it was thick enough to make sugar, she teased Jeff into giving her some of it for sugar snow.

After awhile, Uncle Jack came back from the woods.

"Time for lunch," he told Dot. "Aunt Betty packed enough for an army."

He opened a box and took out sandwiches, cake, apples and other good things. Somehow Dot did not feel hungry. Uncle Jack noticed that she was not eating.

"What's the matter, Dot?" he asked. "Don't tell me that all this work and fresh air hasn't made you hungry?"

The little girl tried to eat her sandwich but it seemed to stick in her throat. She didn't feel very well. The smoke from the fire smarted her eyes, and the odor from the cooking sirup gave her a queer feeling in her stomach.

Dot sat down in a corner. Dash came over

and licked her hand, but she didn't even notice.

"Uncle Jack," she said in a quavering voice. "I think I'm going to be sick."

CHAPTER VIII

INTO THE WOODS

UNCLE JACK laid aside his own lunch and looked at Dot anxiously.

"Why, what is the matter?" he asked.

"I don't know," answered Dot, "unless maybe I ate too much maple sugar."

"Why, two small cakes shouldn't make you ill."

"She's had more than that," said Jeff.

"Oh, yes," Dot agreed. "I had a lot of snow sugar and all the crumbs that broke off the big cakes."

"Then it's no wonder you feel sick and can't eat your lunch," said Uncle Jack. "I think I'll have to take you home."

He carried her out to the bob sled and with Dash snuggled beside her, they started for the house. The little girl thought that the horses traveled very slowly. It seemed to take such a long time to get there.

When Uncle Jack lifted her down from the sled she was feeling much worse.

"O-oh, my stomach feels like I had swallowed a big rock," she moaned.

Aunt Betty came to the door and she looked frightened when she saw Dot.

"Why, what is the matter with the child?" she cried. "She hasn't been hurt?"

"She ate too much maple sugar," explained Uncle Jack as he carried her into the kitchen.

"Oh, the poor little dear," murmured Aunt Betty. "Take her into the bedroom, Jack. You shouldn't have allowed her to gorge herself!"

"It wasn't Uncle Jack's fault," Dot said loyally. "He thought I had eaten only two tiny cakes."

"Aunt Betty will fix you up, dear. Now don't try to talk. Just lie still."

In a very few minutes the little girl had been undressed and put to bed. A hot water bottle was placed at her feet and another one at her stomach. Aunt Betty gave her a spoonful of black, bitter medicine which was very hard to take.

"There now," Aunt Betty said as she tucked in the covers. "That ought to make you feel better."

Dot soon dropped off into a deep slumber. She would have slept until dinner time had she not been aroused by a crashing thump on the bed. She opened her eyes and there was Dash! His nose was almost in her face.

"Get down, Dash!" she cried, trying to push him away. "You'll get the covers all dirty."

Dash paid no attention. Instead, he tried to remove the covers from his little mistress by digging at them with his front paws.

"Why, Dash, you bad dog," Dot scolded. She seized his collar and pushed him right off the bed.

The little girl was thoroughly awake now. For a moment she couldn't remember why she was in bed during the daytime. Then she recalled that it was because she had eaten too much maple sugar.

"I feel all right now," she thought. "My stomach doesn't ache a bit."

Dash was pulling at the covers again so Dot decided to get up and dress. As she flung back the covers, one of the hot water bottles fell to the floor. Dash was on it in a flash. He seized the rubber bag in his teeth and shook it as if it were a rat.

"Drop that, Dash!" Dot ordered sternly. "Drop it!"

Dash shook the bottle all the harder. His sharp teeth went through the rubber and a stream of water poured into his mouth and out on the floor.

"Oh! Oh! Now see what you've done!" Dot scolded. "You've ruined Aunt Betty's hot water bottle!"

She picked up the rubber bag and hurried with it to the bathroom. There she drained the rest of the water into the wash basin.

"Such a dog I never saw," Dot said. "I hope Aunt Betty won't be cross about this."

Before going down to the kitchen she took a towel and wiped up the water on the bedroom floor. She had seen Mrs. Green do this when liquids were spilled. It kept the woodwork from spotting.

Aunt Betty was very nice about the hot water bottle when Dot told her what had happened.

"It doesn't matter," she said. "The bag was an old one. That's probably why it broke so easily. Dogs will be dogs."

Aunt Betty was glad to see that Dot was feeling better.

"Supper soon will be ready," she told the little girl. "Shall I set a place for you?"

"Oh, yes," replied Dot. "You see, I haven't eaten a thing since breakfast—that is, except maple sugar."

A few minutes later Uncle Jack came stamping in out of the snow and Jeff was with him. They both asked how Dot felt and talked with her while Aunt Betty cooked the meal.

"Uncle Jack, may I go with you to the shack tomorrow?"

"Well, now, that depends," he replied

slowly. "Will you promise not to eat too much sugar?"

"I don't think I'll want even a tiny cake," Dot said soberly. "It's too sweet."

"You feel that way because you had too much of it at one time," laughed Uncle Jack. "Our maple sugar is really very good. And so is our sirup. It's the very best in the county."

"That's only our opinion," said Aunt Betty from the kitchen. "Others don't seem to think so, for it's never won a prize."

"We'll win one this year!" Uncle Jack exclaimed. "Our sirup will be the best we've ever made!"

Dot did not understand what they meant until Aunt Betty told her that each year the maple growers held a festival in the village. Judges tested a sample of sirup submitted by each farmer, and the best was awarded a prize.

"The honor means a great deal," explained Aunt Betty. "Folks always want to buy a sirup which has been given an award, and they're willing to pay fancy prices for it."

"Betty has set her heart on winning the prize this year," said Uncle Jack. "We came close to it last season."

Supper was ready at last and Dot ate her share. She was glad that Aunt Betty had not cooked any sweet things.

After the dishes were washed, Uncle Jack turned on the radio. They listened to a program of music which came from Dot's own town of Fremont. Somehow it made her think of her mother and father. She missed them dreadfully and wondered what they had been doing while she was away.

"Aunt Betty, will I get a letter tomorrow?" she asked suddenly.

"From your parents, dear? Why, I think you might, only it takes a long while for mail to travel up here."

After awhile, Dot went off to bed, but she could not go to sleep. She felt so lonesome for her mother. She kept thinking about Roger too and wondering if he had forgotten to feed the peacock. Fremont seemed so far away.

Salty tears began to trickle down Dot's cheek. She brushed them away and burrowed deep into the covers so that Aunt Betty wouldn't hear her cry. She just couldn't let anyone know that she was homesick.

The morning sun was streaming in at the window when Dot awoke. She sat up and looked around. It was very late she knew.

Scratch! Scratch!

Dot heard the sound at her bedroom door. She ran to open it. Dash leaped into the room and gave a little bark as much as to say: "It's *time* you're getting up!"

Dot dressed as quickly as she could and hurried down to the kitchen.

"Good morning, dear," said Aunt Betty. "How do you feel?"

"Oh, just fine, Aunt Betty. What time is it?"

"Ten o'clock. I let you sleep late on purpose."

"Has Uncle Jack gone to the sugar camp?" Dot asked anxiously.

"Oh, yes, hours ago."

"Then I won't get to help him make sirup." Dot felt very badly because she had overslept.

"Jack will come back for you at noon," Aunt Betty smiled.

She gave Dot her breakfast. While the little girl ate at the table by the window, she saw a man drive up in an old muddy car. He stopped beside a tin box which was perched on a post, and dropped something into it.

"Who is that, Aunt Betty?" asked Dot.

"Why, it's the mailman," replied Aunt Betty. "He's left us something too."

"Maybe he brought me a letter!" cried Dot. She could not eat any more breakfast, so Aunt Betty let her run out to look in the mailbox.

There were three letters, but Dot's name was not on any of them. She was disappointed enough to cry.

"Now don't you fret, dear," said Aunt

Betty, taking the little girl into her lap. "You'll get a letter soon I know. After all, you've only been here two days."

Dot tried to play with Imogene but Dash seemed to be jealous. Whenever she held the doll he would try to squeeze in between them.

Suddenly the telephone rang and Aunt Betty went to answer it. Her face was beaming when she turned back to look at Dot.

"Oh, it's good news!" she exclaimed. "A telegram from your father!"

"From Daddy?" Dot cried, springing to her feet. "But Aunt Betty, telegrams come in envelopes."

"This one was telephoned from the Mapletown station. You father wires that the operation was successful! Your mother will be well in a very few weeks, Dot!"

"You mean she'll be all cured, Aunt Betty? So she can play with me again?"

"Yes!" laughed Aunt Betty, and she gave Dot a happy squeeze. "I'm so glad I could cry!"

Dot felt as if a great load had been lifted from her own mind. Of course she had known that Daddy would make things come out right, but it had seemed to take such a long time.

Aunt Betty sang as she worked in the kitchen and when Uncle Jack came home for lunch, she told him the good news. Dot noticed that they were both so much more cheerful.

"Want to come with me to the sugar camp?" asked Uncle Jack. "I need an extra helper this afternoon."

"Oh, I want to help," cried Dot, and she ran to find her boots.

Uncle Jack had not driven the horses back to the house. He took Dot's hand, and with Dash trotting at their heels, set off afoot through the field. The snow was melting fast but there were a few large drifts left. Dash did not like to wade through them. He would whine and then Uncle Jack would carry him.

"This pup is more bother than he's worth," he complained jokingly.

At the camp, Dot watched Jeff making maple sirup. She did not need to be told to stay away from the tubs of sugar. She even shook her head when Uncle Jack offered her a taste of newly made sirup.

Dot helped to empty the small buckets of sap from the trees close to the cabin. After awhile she thought she would like to explore the woods in the opposite direction. She walked slowly along, stopping now and then to peer down into one of the sap buckets. None of them was full enough to need emptying.

Soon there were no more maple trees. Dot thought she would turn back but just then Dash darted off into the timber after a squirrel.

Dot was afraid the little dog would get lost so she followed as fast as she could. She was so busy watching Dash that she scarcely noticed how dark it had grown. The trees grew closer and closer together, and the under-brush became dense.

"Come here, Dash!" called Dot.

The terrier came trotting back and looked at her questioningly.

"It's time for us to go back," Dot told him. "Uncle Jack may be ready to start home."

They set off through the trees, but some-how the trail didn't look the same. Dot was not just sure where she would find the sugar house for she couldn't see the smoke from its chimney. If Dash hadn't been with her she might have been frightened. As it was, she was only a little bit uneasy.

Dot felt better when she came to a trail which was clearly marked.

"We're all right now, Dash," she said. "This will take us back to the sugar house."

She started down the trail. Before she had taken many steps, Dash came running after her. He caught her dress in his strong teeth and began pulling.

"Stop that, Dash!" Dot cried, trying to

jerk away. "I don't want to play with you now."

Dash didn't seem in a very playful mood. He held fast to Dot's clothing, only letting go of it long enough to bark.

The little girl pulled away from him, but when she tried to run, Dash was right there again, pulling at her dress. He was very strong.

Dot began to grow frightened for it was almost dark.

"Let me go, Dash!" she pleaded, very close to tears. "Please let me go, or we'll never get back to the sugar camp!"

CHAPTER IX

The Roadside Stand

DASH would not obey his little mistress. He kept tugging at her dress and barking excitedly. It was his way of trying to tell her that she had taken the wrong trail.

"Oh, Dash! You're a bad, wicked dog!" Dot cried, and by this time tears of vexation were streaming down her cheeks.

She picked up a stick, intending to switch the terrier lightly on the legs. He sidled away but would not let go of her dress. He tried to pull her back toward the other trail.

Just then Dot heard Uncle Jack's voice. He was calling to her from a long distance away.

"Oh, Uncle Jack! Uncle Jack!" she shouted. "Come here and help me."

In a minute her uncle came hurrying into view. He looked worried and was all out of breath from running.

"Oh, here you are, Dot!" he exclaimed in relief.

"Dash is a bad dog, Uncle Jack! Make him let me go!"

Now that help was at hand, the terrier no longer tugged at Dot's dress. He released his hold and trotted over to Uncle Jack, looking up at him pleadingly.

"Good dog!" said Uncle Jack, and gave him a pat.

"I don't think he's good for anything," said Dot crossly. "He chews up hats, and breaks hot water bottles. Now he's torn a big hole in my dress and I won't be able to wear it anymore."

"He saved you from taking the wrong trail," replied Uncle Jack quietly. "Dash knew that this wasn't the way back to the sugar house. That's why he tried to hold you and bark for help."

"Doesn't this path lead back to the camp, Uncle Jack?" Dot was very much surprised.

"No, it goes down to the river. If you had

gone that way I don't know how long it would have taken us to find you."

"Were you looking for me, Uncle Jack?" Dot asked.

"Yes, I was worried when I noticed by your tracks in the snow that you had gone this way. I knew you would soon lose yourself in the woods."

"I'm sorry I went off from the sugar camp," Dot said. "I only meant to walk a little way."

"After this you must stay close to the shack," Uncle Jack cautioned her. "It's easy to get lost. If I hadn't heard Dash barking, I might not have found you for hours."

Dot reached down to pet the terrier. She was sorry that she had switched him even a tiny bit, but of course she had not understood. Dash quivered with pleasure and licked her hand. He was glad that she liked him again.

"It's time we're starting for home," said

Uncle Jack. "Aunt Betty will be waiting supper for us."

Dot was so tired she could not walk very fast. Uncle Jack lifted her in his arms and carried her all the way back to the sugar camp. In the bob-sled riding home, the little girl fell asleep.

"Wake up," said Uncle Jack a few minutes later. "We're here."

He carried her into the house where Aunt Betty was frying doughnuts.

"Too much maple sugar *again?*" she asked, letting her big spoon clatter on the stove.

"No, only a very tired little girl this time," replied Uncle Jack. "She lost herself in the woods."

"And Dash saved me," Dot added drowsily.

When Aunt Betty had heard the story, she gave the terrier a large plate of food as his reward for a good deed.

"I think it's just as well that the sugar

season is about ended," she told Dot as she
helped undress her for bed. "I declare, I'm
afraid we'll never get you back to Fremont
safe and healthy."

"Dash will look after me," the little girl
mumbled just before she went off to sleep.

In the morning Dot did not go to the sugar
camp, and by nightfall Uncle Jack reported
that the sap had practically ceased to flow.

"Today will end the work," he told Aunt
Betty.

"Have you heard when the maple festival
is to be held?" she asked.

"Yes, it will be late next week," Uncle
Jack replied.

"Are we going?" inquired Dot eagerly.

"Oh, we never miss a maple festival,"
laughed Aunt Betty. "This year I hope our
sirup will win the first prize. It's the best
sirup we've ever made."

"Other folks are turning out good sirup
too," said Uncle Jack teasingly.

The next afternoon Dot helped her aunt
wrap the packages of maple sugar which

were to be sent to Fremont and New York.
When the rural mailman drove by in his bat-
tered old car, they gave the parcels to him.

In return the man handed them several
letters. Dot received a long one from her
Daddy in New York, and another from Mrs.
Green. She could read them both because
the words were all short and easy. Daddy's
letter was especially nice for he had drawn
funny little men all over the margins.

"Mother is getting better every day," Dot
told Aunt Betty. "My peacock is all right
too. Roger didn't forget to feed him."

The little girl wanted to answer both letters so Aunt Betty gave her writing paper
and a fountain pen. It took her a long while
to write a few lines to her father, and just
as she was signing her name at the end, she
spilled a huge drop of ink on the paper.

"Oh, dear, now I've ruined it."

"I don't believe your father will mind the
blot," said Aunt Betty. "I'd send it along
that way since you've worked so hard."

"I am pretty tired," sighed Dot. "I

guess I'll wait until tomorrow to write Mrs. Green."

She marked a long row of X X X's across the bottom of the page which were kisses for her mother. Then she sealed the letter and stamped it.

The next morning at the breakfast table, Uncle Jack remarked that it was time to open up the roadside stand.

"Oh, are you going to sell vegetables?" Dot asked eagerly. She had seen many such stands along the country roads near Fremont.

"It's too early for many vegetables," laughed Uncle Jack. "We'll sell jugs of maple sirup."

"This would be a nice day to start," nodded Aunt Betty. "The weather is warm and there should be quite a number of cars on the road."

"I'll get busy right away," promised Uncle Jack.

He took Dot and Dash with him when he went down to the main road to look at the stand which he had built the previous spring. To reach it they cut through the meadow and walked down over a hill.

"Why don't you have your stand right in front of the house?" asked Dot. "They have them that way in Fremont."

"We'd like it better ourselves," replied Uncle Jack. "But very little traffic passes on the side road. The tourists all take the main highway and they are the ones who buy our sugar."

The stand was similar to others which Dot had seen. It had a wooden counter and a roof to keep out the rain.

Uncle Jack had brought a bucket of water and some old rags. He washed the stained counter and tacked a strip of white oilcloth over it. While he worked several cars went past.

"Now we're all ready to bring down our cans of sirup," Uncle Jack declared. "We'll not do that until after lunch."

In the afternoon, Aunt Betty went with them to look at the stand. She carried a

smiled too because she wanted the customer to buy some of the sirup.

"How much is your maple sugar?" asked the lady.

"Twenty-five cents each for the cakes," replied Aunt Betty.

"And your sirup?"

"Seventy-five cents for the little jug. A dollar seventy for the large can."

"Oh, dear," said the lady, "Vermont prices are *so* high."

"It requires a great deal of work to make maple sirup and sugar," explained Aunt Betty politely.

"I'm sure it does," agreed the lady, "but I don't believe I'll buy anything this time."

She went back to her car and drove away.

"Aunt Betty, maybe we ought to sell our sirup cheaper," Dot said anxiously. "Is it too high?"

"I don't think so," replied Aunt Betty. "There are always a certain number of people who would not buy at any price."

After awhile another automobile stopped

in front of the stand.   This time the lady and man did not even get out.   They just called to ask Aunt Betty the price of her wares, and then said they would take a small jug of sirup.   Dot carried it out to them and they gave her the exact change.

"Well, we've made our first sale," declared Aunt Betty.   "I doubt that business will be very brisk today."

During the next hour they sold one large can of sirup, three glasses of jelly and two cakes of sugar.

"I'd like to run up to the house and get another ball of yarn," said Aunt Betty. "Do you want to tend the stand for a few minutes?"

"Oh, yes!" cried Dot.   "I'll look after it while you're gone."

Aunt Betty walked through the meadow toward the house.   Dot began to watch the road anxiously.   How proud she would be if she could sell something while her Aunt was away!

One car after another whizzed past, and

then a large blue one slowed up as it drew near the stand.

"It's going to stop!" Dot thought excitedly.

The car halted on the opposite side of the road. A tall man in a gray tweed suit stepped down and walked over to the stand.

"Well, well, are you in charge, young lady?" he asked.

"Yes, sir," said Dot. "Would you like some nice maple sugar?"

"No, I think I'd prefer to have some sirup," answered the man, smiling at her.

"The little jugs are seventy-five cents," Dot told him.

"I'll need a large can. How much are they?"

Dot reached down behind the counter and lifted out one of the heavy containers. The man helped her with it.

"These cans cost a dollar something," Dot said vaguely. "I can't remember how many cents."

"Isn't your mother here?"

"Oh, no, she's in New York."

"Then who runs this stand?" asked the man.

"My Aunt Betty. She went up to the house for a ball of yarn."

"Do you suppose you could run and get her? I'd like to have this sirup."

"I'll bring her right away," Dot promised.

She untied Dash's leash and together they raced up the hill.

"Aunt Betty! Aunt Betty!" she cried shrilly, flinging open the kitchen door.

There was no answer. Dot ran from room to room but she could not find her aunt anywhere. Finally she went back out doors. Then she caught sight of Aunt Betty down by the barn feeding the chickens.

Dot ran to tell her about the stranger who wished to buy a can of sirup.

"Why, the price is a dollar and seventy cents a gallon," Aunt Betty said. "I'll wash my hands and come right down."

Dot and Dash did not wait but ran back to tell the stranger that Aunt Betty would come in a minute.

"Why, where is he?" gasped Dot as she reached the stand.

Both the man and his car had disappeared.

CHAPTER X

AUNT BETTY'S LOSS

Dot looked up and down the road but she could not see the automobile anywhere. Then she stared at the counter and made an alarming discovery. The can of maple sirup was missing.

"The man must have carried it away with him!" Dot thought.

Just at that moment Aunt Betty came hurrying out.

"He didn't wait," Dot told her excitedly.

"Well, that's just too bad after you made a special trip to get me," said Aunt Betty. "After this, Dot, you shouldn't leave the stand unless you take the money box with you."

The little girl had forgotten all about the box of change under the counter.

"Oh, Aunt Betty," she stammered, "maybe it's gone now."

"No, I don't think so," laughed Aunt Betty. "Most folks are honest."

"But the can of sirup is missing."

"A can of sirup?" Aunt Betty echoed. Quickly she bent down to look under the counter. "Why, you're right. One is gone! And I don't believe the man left any money to pay for it."

She and Dot searched carefully on the counter. They could not find any money.

"It's a wonder he didn't steal more than one can of sirup," said Aunt Betty crossly. "Thank goodness the box of change is still here."

She counted the silver coins to make certain that none had been taken.

"I don't suppose the man took time to look under the counter," Aunt Betty said. "He probably picked up the one can and drove off as fast as he could."

Dot felt very badly over the loss of the sirup. She asked Aunt Betty if it were her fault.

"No, dear, you had no way of knowing the man was dishonest. Tell me, what did he look like?"

"He wore a gray suit," replied Dot, thinking very hard. "He seemed real friendly too."

"Can't you remember anything more about him?"

"He had a big blue car and one of the fenders was dented."

"So many folks have cars like that and wear gray suits," sighed Aunt Betty.

"If he ever stops here again I'll remember him."

"The man will not be foolish enough to do that," replied Aunt Betty. "No, our sirup is gone. But after this, we must watch the stand more closely."

Dot helped her Aunt carry the heavy cans back to the house, for it was too late to sell any more sirup that day. At the supper table, Uncle Jack heard all about what had happened.

"We can't afford to lose many cans of sirup or all our profit soon will be gone," he remarked.

Although neither Aunt Betty nor Uncle Jack thought that Dot had been at fault, the little girl blamed herself. She should never have left the stand. Why hadn't she remembered the price of the sirup? Then there would have been no need to run to the house after Aunt Betty.

"I'll watch for the man," she promised soberly. "When I see him again I'll call a policeman!"

"We haven't any policemen up here," laughed Uncle Jack. "Don't worry about the maple sirup, Dot. We'll forget all about it."

During the next few days, Dot spent many hours at the roadside stand with her aunt. The weather had turned warmer. With the last of the snow gone, more cars passed on the road. Business became fairly brisk and several people drove all the way from Maple-town just to buy sirup from Aunt Betty.

"It's the best in the county," declared one man as he carried two large square cans to his car. "I'd drive fifty miles to buy it."

"I hope the judges at the festival hold the same opinion," laughed Aunt Betty.

Dot kept close watch of every car which went down the road. One afternoon she saw an automobile which she felt certain belonged to the man who had taken the sirup.

"Oh, there he is, Aunt Betty!" she shouted.

The car slowed down, and then Dot knew that it wasn't the same man at all. He was riding with a little girl who looked to be her own age.

"Why, that is our neighbor, Mr. Brighton," chuckled Aunt Betty. "He has his daughter, Mary, with him."

Mr. Brighton stopped the car to chat for a moment with Aunt Betty. He said he was on his way to Mapletown to buy supplies.

"Why don't you leave Mary here until you come back?" invited Aunt Betty. "She could play with Dot."

"Yes, please let me stay," Mary coaxed her father. She was a pretty little girl with brown eyes and dark hair which she wore in two braids tied with red ribbon.

"All right," agreed Mr. Brighton, "but mind you don't get into any mischief."

It did not take Dot and Mary long to become acquainted. They played with Imogene and raced back and forth with Dash. Dot felt very proud because the terrier would sit up and slowly roll over when she commanded him.

"My dog's name is Shep," Mary said. "He can drive the cows, but he doesn't know any tricks."

Dot told her visitor about the man who had taken Aunt Betty's maple sirup from the roadside stand.

"My mother has a stand too," Mary declared. "But no one ever stole anything from her."

"I must find the thief before I go back to Fremont. I keep watching and watching for him."

"I'll help you," promised Mary. "And so will my brothers, Jerry and Fred."

While Dot was telling her little friend how the man had driven away in a large blue car with a dented fender, Aunt Betty called from the stand.

"Mary, your father is here!"

"I'll have to go now," the little girl said hurriedly. "Come over and see me soon."

"I will if Aunt Betty says I may. Don't forget to watch for the thief who ran off with our sirup!"

After Mary had gone, Dot felt rather lonely. She sat beside Aunt Betty at the stand, watching her knit a sweater. It was not very exciting when folks did not stop to buy their wares.

Glancing up the side road which led to the house, Dot saw Uncle Jack and Jeff coming with the team and lumber wagon.

"Oh, Aunt Betty, are they going to town?" she asked eagerly.

"No, only into the timber to saw wood. Would you like to go with them?"

Dot thought that it would be fun to ride with Uncle Jack. With Dash scampering at her heels, she ran down the road to signal him.

"Whoa there!" said Uncle Jack, pulling on the reins. "What's wrong now, Dot?"

"Aunt Betty says I can go with you to saw wood!"

"Well, well," laughed Uncle Jack, as he reached down and hauled her up into the wagon. "Jeff and I need a little helper."

He clucked to the horses and they went on down the road. Dot snuggled close beside her uncle.

"May I hold the reins?" she asked.

Uncle Jack laid them in her hands. At first Dot was afraid that the horses might run away so she held the reins tightly.

"Loosen them a bit," said Uncle Jack, "or the horses will think you want them to stop."

After a few minutes Dot did not feel nervous about driving. She began to wish that the team would go faster.

"Giddap!" she shouted, slapping the horses' backs with the reins as she had seen Uncle Jack do. "Giddap, Maud!"

They paid no attention at all, but kept plodding slowly along.

"I guess the horses are pretty tired to-day," sighed Dot.

A moment later Uncle Jack took the reins and turned the team into a side road. Jeff sprang out of the wagon to open a gate. The wagon passed through into a dense timber.

"This is the end of the line," declared Uncle Jack. "Everyone out!"

He jumped down to the ground with the reins still in his hands. Dash leaped after him, but Dot waited until Jeff helped her for she might have been hurt.

Uncle Jack tied the horses to a tree. Then he and Jeff took their cross-cut saw from the wagon and walked a little way up the road.

"This looks like a good tree," said Uncle Jack, pointing to a tall, straight pine which stood in an open spot. "It will be easy to get."

Dot sat down on a stump to watch Jeff and her uncle work. One of them stood on each side of the tree, and they made their sharp-tooth saw go back and forth into the trunk with a whirring noise.

"Don't come too close," Uncle Jack warned as Dot moved near. "You might get hurt."

After awhile, the men grew tired and sat down to rest.

"I wish I had a drink of water," said Jeff. "We should have brought a jug with us."

"There is a glass in the wagon," replied Uncle Jack. "And the spring is up the road only a little ways."

"Oh, I can do without a drink," said Jeff. "We ought to get on with the sawing."

"I'll bring you some water, Jeff," Dot declared eagerly. She wanted to help.

"Do you think you could find the spring

without getting lost?" asked Uncle Jack with a twinkle in his eye.

"Oh, yes, I'll take Dash with me. He'll remember the way."

"The spring is not hard to find," Uncle Jack told her. "It's only up the road a short distance. You'll see a pipe coming out of a rock. Just fill the glass and bring it back."

"Don't leave the road at all," cautioned Jeff. "The spring is on the right hand side."

"I'll find it," Dot declared.

Uncle Jack gave her the drinking glass and told her not to drop it. She called Dash, and together they ran down the road. A sharp bend soon hid them from view of the wagon, but Dot was not afraid she would get lost this time.

A little farther on she came to the spring. A stream of water was gushing out of a pipe by the side of the road. Dot filled her glass and drank deeply. The water was icy cold but oh, so good!

She rinsed out the glass and filled it again for Jeff. Then she carefully picked her way over the rocks lest she fall and spill all the water.

For no reason at all, or so it seemed to Dot, the terrier began to bark.

"Oh, do be quiet, Dash!"

Dot glanced up to see if the dog was teasing another squirrel. She stopped short and stared.

There in front of her, not a dozen yards away was an animal which she had never seen before. It was small and dark and covered with long, sharp spines.

Dot gave a cry of terror and started to run.

CHAPTER XI

A BALL OF QUILLS

DOT was so startled that her one thought was to get away. As she ran, she looked back over her shoulder. Dash was carrying on at a great rate, barking and making savage little darts toward the quilled creature.

"Dash! Dash!" she called. Dot was afraid the animal might attack him.

In her anxiety the little girl did not notice where she was going. She stumbled over a stone and fell to the ground. The glass slipped from her hand, and striking the rock, shattered into a dozen pieces. Her mittens were soaked with water.

"Oh! Oh!" wailed Dot, struggling to her feet again.

She ran as fast as she could down the road.

"Uncle Jack! Uncle Jack!" she cried,

151

coming within view of the lumber wagon.

Both Jeff and her uncle came hurrying out from the timber. Dot had never seen them so excited.

"Stand right where you are!" shouted Uncle Jack. "Don't move!"

The next moment, before Dot had time to realize what was wrong, a great tree shivered and sighed. She glanced up and saw its branches trembling and dancing. Then with a mighty crash it fell to earth only a little distance from where she was standing.

Uncle Jack came running toward Dot. He caught her in his arms.

"You gave me a fright that time," he declared. "The tree didn't fall just as we planned, and I thought you'd run straight into its path. Don't tremble so, Dot. There's nothing to be afraid of now."

"I'm not 'fraid of the tree," the little girl cried. "It's the animal at the spring! Oh, Uncle Jack, he meant to bite me!"

"There aren't any really wild animals in

this forest," he told her kindly. "Why, your knees are all skinned!"

Dot had not even noticed the jagged holes in her stockings.

"I fell down and broke the glass," she replied, looking at her wound. "I must have hurt myself then."

Uncle Jack made a dressing from a clean handkerchief and placed it under her stocking.

"That will keep the dirt out of the cut. When we get home Aunt Betty will bandage it up properly."

Dot was not worried about her bruised knee. It did feel a little bit stiff when she walked, but she wouldn't have noticed it at all if Uncle Jack hadn't mentioned it.

"I'm afraid Dash will be bitten by that animal," she said anxiously.

"Didn't he follow you back?" Uncle Jack asked looking down the winding trail.

"Oh, no, he was very angry at the little animal. He barked and barked and wouldn't come when I called him."

Uncle Jack's face became grave.

"What kind of an animal was it, Dot?" he inquired.

"There were a lot of big wooden darning needles sticking out of him."

"Why, you must have seen a porcupine, Dot! If Dash attacks him, it will be good-bye dog!"

Without waiting to hear more, Uncle Jack started down the trail toward the spring. His steps were so long that Dot had trouble keeping up with him. But she was so anxious about Dash she didn't even think about being out of breath. If only they could reach the spring before the animal harmed her pet!

"Do porcupines eat dogs when they get angry?" she called to her uncle.

"No, they stick them full of sharp quills if the dog attacks them."

Dash full of quills! The very thought of such a thing made the little girl shudder. She knew how badly it hurt when one ran a sliver into his hand. How much more painful it would be for Dash, if the porcupine peppered him with sharp barbs.

As they drew near the spring, Dot heard Dash barking excitedly. She knew then that he was still alive but he might be hurt.

"Oh, hurry! Hurry, Uncle Jack," Dot urged.

When they reached the spring, Dash was nowhere in sight. They could hear him barking in a dense clump of trees a short distance away. Uncle Jack caught up a heavy stick and ran in that direction.

"I believe he has him treed!" he exclaimed.

"Why, Dash can't climb a tree, Uncle Jack."

"A porcupine can," he replied tersely.

Following the sound of the dog's frenzied barking, they came to a low tree whose main trunk forked into two branches close to the ground. There in the crotch sat the porcupine. He was looking down at Dash who ran first to one side of the tree and then the other. He seemed to be afraid his quarry would get away unless he could be in several places at the same time.

Uncle Jack seized him by the collar.

"Dash, you're a reckless dog," Dot scolded. "You're lucky to be alive. That porcupine might have stuck you so full of quills you'd have died before we could get you to the doctor."

If Dash understood, he did not let on. He lunged toward the tree and kept right on barking. Uncle Jack had to hold him in his arms.

"Come on now, young fellow," he said. "Porcupines are a good thing for you to leave alone."

Uncle Jack started back to the spring but Dash did not wish to be carried away. He whined and looked appealingly at his little mistress as if he wanted her to give him another chance at the porcupine.

When they reached the fallen tree where Jeff was working, Uncle Jack let Dash down on the ground. He ran this way and that with his nose to the ground.

"Yes, Uncle Jack. It looks like a little tombstone."

"Well, that's just what it is. You're looking at the grave of poor old Mike, our shepherd dog. I up-ended that stone for a marker."

"What made him die, Uncle Jack?"

"Mike foolishly attacked a porcupine. He got quills all over his body, even in his mouth and throat. We couldn't pull all of them out and one day he died."

"How terrible," Dot said with a shiver. She hugged Dash close to her.

"You see," Uncle Jack told her soberly, "A wise dog leaves a porcupine alone."

Then he clucked to the horses and they drove slowly home.

CHAPTER XII

AT THE MAPLE FESTIVAL

"DOT, how would you like to visit Mary to-day?" asked Aunt Betty the next morning at the breakfast table. "Your uncle and I are driving over to Mapletown. We could drop you off at the Brighton's."

"Oh, I'd like that!" Dot cried. She wanted to see her little friend again.

Aunt Betty finished the dishes, and then while Uncle Jack was getting the car, she carried out several cans of sirup from the shed.

"Are you going to take those down to the stand?" inquired Dot.

"No, we're taking them to Mapletown to trade for groceries," Aunt Betty explained. "But here is one can which won't be sold."

"What will you do with it, Aunt Betty?"

"We're entering this sample in the maple sirup contest."

162

"Today isn't the festival?" Dot asked in alarm. She certainly didn't want to miss *that*.

"Oh, no," replied Aunt Betty, "the festival starts day after tomorrow. But all the farmers will bring in their samples of sirup today. Then the judges will examine them very carefully, and announce the prize awards at the festival Friday."

"I hope your sirup wins first place!" cried Dot.

"So do I, dear. Our sirup is nice and heavy this year, and the flavor is especially good."

As Dot followed her aunt down to the gate, the latter explained that the quality of maple sirup was judged by weight, appearance and flavor.

"Some folks spoil their product by not boiling it long enough," Aunt Betty told the little girl. "Then it usually is light in weight and doesn't look or taste as well."

Uncle Jack came with the car and lifted the heavy cans of sirup into the back seat.

Dash leaped in and found a space for himself by the window. He rode with his forepaws against the glass.

"It looks as if we'll have good weather this week end," remarked Uncle Jack, steering the car down the road. "There should be a large turn-out for the festival."

"We're going, aren't we?" Dot asked anxiously.

"Oh, yes," declared Aunt Betty, "rain or shine we'll take a lunch and spend the day."

The car came to the Brighton farm. Uncle Jack waited in the lane until Dot had made sure that Mary was at home. Then he and Aunt Betty drove on toward Mapletown.

"Hello Dot," said Mary cordially, and she reached down to shake Dash's paw. "Have you found the man who took your aunt's sirup?"

"Not yet," sighed Dot. "I've watched every day but I've never seen the car again."

"I've kept looking too," Mary told her. "I think he must have driven 'way off."

Dot felt very discouraged. She had begun to fear that she would never find the thief.

"Do you want to see my dog?" asked Mary.

She led Dot to the back of the house. Shep was sunning himself on the back porch. He lay with his head on his forepaws, eyes half closed. Dot thought that he looked old and tired. He certainly needed a bath for his long hair was dirty and filled with burrs.

"Here, Shep!" called Mary.

The dog slowly arose to its feet but did not come to her. Then his hair seemed to bristle and he growled.

"Why, Shep, what's the matter?" asked Mary.

Dot turned her head and saw that Dash had followed them around the corner of the house. He was standing perfectly still, looking at Shep.

"Our dogs don't like each other very well," she remarked. "Shep is snarling at Dash."

"Lie down, Shep!" ordered Mary.

The dog did not obey. Instead he suddenly sprang at Dash. Their heads locked together and they rolled over and over, snarling and snapping.

"Oh, make him stop!" screamed Dot. "Shep is killing Dash!"

"Mama! Mama!" shouted Mary.

Mrs. Brighton came running out the back door. She tried to pull the dogs apart. When she could not do that, she caught up a heavy stick and struck Shep sharply on the nose.

He let go his hold. Dot darted forward and snatched Dash away before the fight could start again. The terrier growled and tried to leap from his mistress' arms. He wanted to get at old Shep.

"Be quiet, Dash!" Dot ordered. She gave him a spank, but only a little one, for she did not think the fight had been the terrier's fault.

"Shep is bleeding!" wailed Mary. "Dash chewed a hole in his shoulder!"

"Dash's collar is half torn off," replied Dot.

"Neither of the dogs are really hurt," said Mary's mother. "But they must be kept apart. Shep is getting old and cross. We'll lock him in the barn until he's ready to behave himself."

Dot held Dash while Mrs. Brighton led Shep away. She was glad that her terrier had stood up for his own rights against a much larger dog than himself, but of course she would not wish him to start a fight.

"Do you want to swing?" invited Mary after Dash had quieted down. "My father built one for me in the apple tree."

The swing was a high one, and when Mary pushed, Dot sailed far out toward the garage. She pulled backwards against the ropes to send herself still higher.

"Now let's 'work-up'," said Mary after she had taken her turn.

They stood on the swing board facing each other and holding fast to the ropes. First one would dip and pull, then the other. They kept going higher and higher until they were so tired they had to rest.

"Now I'll whirl you!" cried Mary.

Dot seated herself in the swing while her friend twisted the ropes until she was "wound up." Then Mary gave her a little push and she began to unwind, spinning round and round like a top.

"O-oh," laughed Dot as she staggered to her feet. "I'm dizzy!"

"It's my turn now," cried Mary.

Before she could seat herself in the swing, Mrs. Brighton called from the back porch.

"Dot, your uncle is waiting for you!"

"I'll have to go now," she told Mary. "I've had a nice time and I'm sorry that Dash bit Shep."

"Goodbye, Dot," replied Mary. "Maybe I'll see you at the maple festival."

On the way back to the farm, Uncle Jack and Aunt Betty told the little girl about their trip to Mapletown. They had left their can of maple sirup with the judges of the festival.

"It will be harder than ever to win the prize this year," sighed Aunt Betty. "More than a hundred persons are trying for it."

Dot could hardly wait until Friday. All the next afternoon she lingered in the kitchen while Aunt Betty baked good things to eat. She made a chocolate cake with mounds of white frosting. Dot was allowed to scrape the pan clean.

"We'll need plenty of food for to-morrow," declared Aunt Betty.

Besides the cake, she baked three pans of cookies and made a juicy meat loaf. Then she boiled potatoes to have them all ready for a salad the next morning.

"We'll be starting for Mapletown soon after breakfast," Aunt Betty said. "I want things so I can pop them right into the lunch basket."

"I wish tomorrow would hurry and come," sighed Dot.

In the morning Aunt Betty had breakfast on the table almost before the sun was up. It was not too early for Dot. She couldn't get started for Mapletown quickly enough.

"Maybe we ought to leave Dash here," Aunt Betty said thoughtfully as she finished packing the lunch basket. "There will be a large crowd at the festival. He's apt to be a nuisance."

"Oh, Dash won't be any trouble," Dot told her earnestly.

Aunt Betty smiled and said that he could go along. Uncle Jack brought the car to the gate.

"Don't forget to feed the stock, Jeff, if we get home after dark," he called to the hired man.

"I'll look after everything," promised Jeff. "Have a good time."

It seemed to Dot that it took a long while to drive down the mountain. Several cars went past them and one man tooted his horn at Uncle Jack.

Finally they came to Mapletown and drove slowly around looking for a place to leave the automobile. Cars were parked everywhere. The town square was jammed with people.

"I guess this is as close as we can get," said Uncle Jack.

He squeezed the car in between two others at the curbing.

"Now keep close to me, Dot," cautioned Aunt Betty as they started down the street. "We don't want either you or Dash to get lost."

First they went into a large white building on the north side of the square. In a huge room with tables and shelves they saw all the samples of sirup on display.

"Well, my entry is here all right," said Aunt Betty, "but I won't know until late this afternoon if I've won a prize. I declare, I wish the judging was over now."

Next they went into a room which contained all sorts of old furniture, dishes and odd looking things. "Antiques," Aunt Betty called them but Dot did not find them very interesting.

She was glad when they walked across the square where nearly all the people had gathered. They stopped in at a sugar house built exactly like Uncle Jack's shack in the woods.

The crowd was so great Dot could not get very close to the place where sirup was being made. But in a few minutes a man dipped some of the hot liquid out of the boiler, and ladled it into tiny pans. These he passed out to the crowd. Uncle Jack was able to get one for Dot.

"The sirup is just right to harden now," he told her. "Stir it with this tin spoon."

Dot had forgotten that she had said she did not want any more maple sugar. She had not eaten any for a long while. It would taste good now.

She stirred the sirup in her tiny pan, taking care not to spill a drop of it. When it had hardened and cooled, she politely offered some of the sugar to Aunt Betty and Uncle Jack.

"No, dear, eat it all yourself, if you don't think it will make you ill," said Aunt Betty.

Dot nibbled at the sugar as they walked on toward the far end of the square. There a large fire had been built and over it hung a huge iron kettle.

"What are they doing here?" asked Dot.

"Showing the folks how sugar was made in the old days," replied Uncle Jack. "Wooden sap buckets were used then instead of tin. The sirup was all boiled down over an open fire."

Dot moved closer so that she could see the maple sap bubbling in the kettle. She noticed a round chunk of fat hanging on a string just a little above the liquid. Now and then drops of grease would splash down into the kettle.

"Uncle Jack, what is that thing hanging there?" the little girl asked, deeply puzzled.

"Never saw anything like it at our camp

did you?" he chuckled. "In the early days folks thought a piece of fat would keep the kettle from boiling over. In these times we use better methods."

Dot had grown tired, so she and Aunt Betty sat down on a bench to rest. Uncle Jack looked at his watch and said it was almost time for the woodchopper's contest.

"I'll leave Dash here with you," he declared, handing Dot the leash. "I'm going to try my luck chopping wood."

"We'll be along soon to watch you win some prize money," said Aunt Betty.

She told Dot that Uncle Jack was one of the best wood choppers in the county. Last spring he had won a prize for cutting his log in two quicker than any other person.

The crowd was so great that when Dot and Aunt Betty crossed the square they could not get very close to the woodchoppers. People kept pressing against them and pushing.

Dot had trouble keeping Dash from winding his leash about those who were so close.

He made little darts this way and that trying to get away. He did not like to be hemmed in on all sides.

"Oh, there I can see your Uncle Jack now!" exclaimed Aunt Betty, standing a-tiptoe. "Look at those chips fly!"

Dot tried to see too, and for a minute she forgot about Dash. The leash slipped from her fingers. Before she could snatch it up, the terrier darted through the crowd and was gone.

CHAPTER XIII

LOST IN THE CROWD

"OH, Dash is running away!" Dot exclaimed.

She pushed through the crowd trying to reach the little dog. In her great anxiety she did not hear Aunt Betty calling for her to wait.

Folks were very slow about moving out of the way because they were all trying to watch the woodchoppers. Dot was small enough to squeeze through the gaps but it took Aunt Betty much longer.

"Wait, Dot," she called again. The little girl did not realize how easily they might become separated.

Dot's one thought was to reach Dash. He didn't mean to be mischievous, but whenever she came fairly close to him he would dart away as if it were a game. His leash trailed behind him in the dirt.

"Oh, why doesn't someone try to stop him!" thought Dot.

Finally a kind hearted man caught the leash as the terrier tried to squeeze past him. He held Dash until Dot came up to claim him.

"Oh, thank you, sir," she said to the man.

Dash received a good scolding for running away, and then Dot looked about for Aunt Betty. She couldn't see her anywhere.

"Maybe she's still watching Uncle Jack chop wood," the little girl thought. "I'll go back there."

Carrying Dash in her arms, she tried to push through the crowd again. It was hard for the terrier wriggled and tried to get away. He wanted to run on the ground.

Dot could not remember exactly where she and Aunt Betty had been standing. On all sides she was hemmed in by people, and she could not look over their heads.

Finally, after she had searched for a long time, Dot decided that Aunt Betty must be lost. For a moment she was frightened.

Then she comforted herself with the thought that she could still find Uncle Jack. It ought to be easy to reach him for of course he would be chopping wood.

Dot pushed on again. It wasn't so hard to get through the crowd now because folks were starting to walk away. The wood chopping contest was over but Dot did not learn this until she had reached the front rank of people. She could not see her uncle anywhere.

Now Dot was a sensible little girl. She told herself that if she stood right where she was either Aunt Betty or Uncle Jack would soon find her.

For a long while she and Dash waited, but no one came.

"Maybe Uncle Jack and Aunt Betty went back to the car," Dot thought.

The automobile had been parked a long ways from the square. The little girl remembered that they had walked past the large white building which housed Aunt

Betty's sirup. Dot wasn't sure, but she thought she could go back to the car.

"Come along, Dash," she urged, "We're not lost."

The well-filled picnic basket had been left in the car, Dot recalled. Uncle Jack and Aunt Betty would be sure to return for it at dinner time.

"It must be afternoon now," she thought wearily. "I'm 'most starved."

Dot walked and walked, looking carefully at every car along the curbing. She had never imagined automobiles were so much alike.

Then suddenly the little girl halted. Dash who was trotting ahead on his leash, was brought up short, for he hadn't expected his young mistress to stop so abruptly.

Directly ahead in the doorway of a drugstore stood two men. One of them Dot had never seen before, but she knew the tall man who wore a neat-fitting gray tweed suit. It was the same person who had gone off with Aunt Betty's maple sirup!

If Dot had been home in Fremont she would have called a policeman. There weren't any in Mapletown. The only officer she had seen was a man with a stick who stood on the street corner and showed cars which way to turn.

"Oh, I wish Uncle Jack were here!" thought the little girl.

For the moment she forgot all about being lost. She knew that she had to make the thief pay for the can of sirup he had stolen. Aunt Betty couldn't afford to lose the money which he owed her.

The man had not seen Dot for he was busy talking with his companion. Before the little girl could move toward them, the pair walked rapidly down the street.

"Come on, Dash!" Dot whispered excitedly. She couldn't let the thief get away.

The two men walked so fast that Dot had to run a little to keep up. She could hear them talking.

"I've had enough of the festival," said the man in gray tweed. "I'm getting out right away. I expect to be in New Hampshire by tonight."

So the thief meant to run away! Dot knew that now she must never lose sight of him. If he drove out of the state, then Aunt Betty could never get her money for the stolen jug of sirup.

At the next corner the two men separated. Dot kept on following the man who had stolen the maple sirup. He walked very fast until he came to a large dark blue car. It was the same automobile which had stopped at Aunt Betty's stand.

The man unlocked the door with his keys. Just as he was climbing into the car, he gave a sudden exclamation as if he had forgotten something. Then he turned and went across the street into one of the stores.

Dot waited a long while for him to come back. Finally she led Dash across to the store and looked in through the plate glass window of the shop. She could not see the man anywhere. The only person inside the store was the owner.

"I'm sure he went in there," Dot thought, deeply puzzled.

She stood by the door of the shop for a long while, not knowing what to do. After a little, the owner noticed her and came to ask if there was anything she wanted.

"Did you see a man in a gray suit come in here?" Dot inquired gravely.

"A great many men in gray suits have entered my shop today," answered the storekeeper. "The last person was Mr. Elston, a salesman."

"Does he have a big blue car with a dented fender?"

"Well, now really, I don't know," replied the storekeeper a trifle crossly. He was growing impatient. "What is it you want, little girl? I can't have you standing in my doorway."

Dot led Dash hurriedly away. The storekeeper was staring after them. In another minute he would have started asking questions. Dot didn't want to explain about being lost because then someone would take her away and she wouldn't be able to watch the blue car.

She waited until the shop owner had gone inside the building. Then she led Dash back across the street, taking care to watch out for the autos which were passing.

Dot couldn't understand what had become of the man who had stolen Aunt Betty's maple sirup. She thought probably he had bought something inside the shop and then gone out the side door and walked down another street.

"He'll come back to his car sometime," she told herself. "Dash and I will wait right here for him."

Dot sat down on the running board, but Dash would give her no peace. He kept trying to get away. He tugged at his leash until the little girl lost patience.

"I'm going to shut you up in the car where you can't get away!" she told him severely.

Opening the door, she thrust the terrier into the rear seat. Dash did not like to be confined. First he barked, and when that did not win his freedom, he sat up and begged.

"Oh, Dash, you're a problem dog," sighed Dot.

She opened the car door and climbed in beside him. Dash immediately snuggled up to her, content to remain.

Dot shivered. It was cold even inside the automobile. She was tired and hungry. At breakfast she had been too excited to eat much and now she felt certain it must be long past noon.

Dot did not think of deserting her post. She meant to wait for the man who had taken Aunt Betty's sirup even if he didn't come back for hours. She would ask him to pay the money he owed.

Dot was getting colder every minute. After awhile she moved down into the bottom of the car and pulled a heavy wool

lap robe over her. She felt quite comfortable then.

The delightful warmth made the little
girl feel drowsy. She did not mean to go to
sleep. But it would do no harm just to close
her eyes for a minute. Dash crept close to
her, glad to share the heavy blanket.

Dot fell asleep with her arm about the
dog, and the robe covering them both.

It was nearly dark when the little girl
opened her eyes. She felt a cold wind rush-
ing across her face. For a minute she
couldn't remember where she was.

Dot could hear a humming noise beneath
her. She raised up quickly and looked
about. Why, she was in a moving car! She
could see trees and telephone poles whizzing
past.

Dot was thoroughly awake now. She
twisted around so that she could see the
driver of the car. It was the man in gray—
the person who had taken Aunt Betty's
maple sirup!

CHAPTER XIV

The Runaway Car

BEFORE Dot could say a word or do anything to attract the man's attention, Dash aroused himself. He began to bark.

The driver heard the dog and was startled. He turned his head quickly to glance back over his shoulder.

"Well, what's this?" he exclaimed in astonishment.

His foot went down hard on the brake and the car came to a standstill at the side of the road.

"A little girl and a dog!" he exclaimed again. "Where did you come from?"

"We've been here all the time," Dot told him. She suddenly became very bold. "You're the man who went off with our maple sirup. You owe my Aunt Betty a lot of money."

"Maple sirup!" echoed the man. Then

186

his face changed. "Oh, now I know! You're the little girl who ran the stand near Mapletown. You sold me a can of sirup."

"You didn't pay me for it," Dot told him soberly. "You ran off before my aunt could come. We've been hunting for you ever since."

"I've been looking for you too," the man replied gravely. "I meant to go back and find that stand again, but I couldn't remember where it was located."

Dot didn't know what to say then. She couldn't understand why the man would be unable to find Aunt Betty's place. Everyone knew where it was.

"You see, I didn't know your aunt's name," the man explained. "I had gathered up over fifteen cans of sirup that day and I couldn't even recall which road your farm was located."

"Didn't you pay for any of the sirup?" Dot asked in astonishment.

"Oh, yes, I settled for all of it except the can I took from you. I was in a great hurry when I stopped at your place. I waited as long as I could for you to bring your aunt. Then I decided to take the sirup and come back later to pay for it."

"Folks shouldn't take things without asking first," Dot said, quoting one of Mrs. Green's remarks.

"You're quite right," the man agreed. "I hope you'll not send me to jail."

"Oh, no," replied Dot, "not if you pay Aunt Betty the money."

"That's right," smiled the man, "I almost forgot again. Let me see, how much was the sirup?"

"A dollar and seventy cents." Dot knew the price very well by this time.

The man whose name was John Elston, opened his wallet and took out a roll of bills. Dot had never seen so much money before.

"Here is two dollars," he said. "That ought to settle my debt with interest."

"What is interest?" Dot asked curiously.

"In this case it's thirty cents which should buy you some candy."

"I like candy," said Dot, "but I'd rather have a sandwich. I'm so hungry, and Dash hasn't had anything to eat either."

"It's my turn to ask questions," said Mr. Elston, looking worried. "How long have you been in my car? And when did you climb in here?"

Dot told him how she and Dash had been separated from Uncle Jack and Aunt Betty at the Maple festival. She explained that they had crawled into the car to wait until Mr. Elston returned.

"Then I've hauled you all the way from Mapletown!" the man exclaimed. "It's nearly five o'clock now. No wonder you're hungry!"

"Aunt Betty will be hunting for me," Dot said anxiously. "I ought to find her right away."

"Young lady, we're easily two hundred miles from Mapletown. You've put me in a nice situation. I'm apt to be accused of kidnaping!"

"I didn't mean to go to sleep."

"It's queer I failed to see you in the car," Mr. Elston declared. "I guess you and the dog were buried under the robe. I don't know what to do with you now."

Dot remained silent. She was without a single idea herself.

"Well, there's nothing to do but drive back to Mapletown," the man said after a moment of thought. "But first, we'll get you something to eat."

"Dash is hungry too," Dot told him.

"The pup looks pretty well fed to me," replied Mr. Elston, "but we'll get him a can of meat somewhere along the line. Come on up front here."

He helped Dot climb over the seat. Then he backed the car around and started toward Mapletown again.

"Better give me that two dollars to keep for you," he advised Dot. "In another minute it will fly out the window and you'll lose it."

The little girl was very glad to return it to him. By this time she liked Mr. Elston a great deal and she was sure he had not meant to steal Aunt Betty's sirup.

"I intended to go back to Mapletown and try to locate your aunt sometime next week," the man explained as he steered the car. "Maybe it's just as well that I see her today. I have an important reason for wishing to talk with her."

"Is it about the sirup?" Dot asked curiously.

Mr. Elston nodded his head. He gave the steering wheel a whirl and the car turned in at a filling station. Beside it was a cafe.

"We'll go in here and get you something to eat, Dot," he declared.

Dogs were not allowed inside the building but Mr. Elston arranged to have food brought out to Dash. Dot felt very grown up as she sat across the table from her new friend.

"See anything you want on the menu?" he asked.

Dot pretended to read the printed card which the waitress had given her.

"I think I'll take some chocolate ice cream," she said.

"Isn't it too cold for that?" asked the man, smiling broadly. "Besides, ice cream isn't very filling when you're hungry."

"Perhaps I could have several dishes of it."

"We might compromise on one for dessert," Mr. Elston said. "Let me see, I think we'll have mashed potatoes and green peas, and how about a little chicken?"

Dot nodded eagerly. She hadn't thought about chicken because at home it was never served except on Sunday.

While the little girl ate her dinner, she told Mr. Elston about the interesting things she had seen at the festival. He asked her many questions, especially about her uncle's maple sugar camp.

"Aunt Betty's sirup is the best around," Dot told him proudly. "Some folks don't boil their sirup enough, but we boil and boil ours."

"I know one thing," declared Mr. Elston. "Your sirup *is* the best in the county, for I believe I've sampled them all."

Dot looked up from her dish of ice cream. She asked gravely:

"And didn't it make you sick, eating all that sirup?"

"No," laughed Mr. Elston, "I only took a very small sample of each."

He arose and looked at the clock on the wall.

"We'll have to be hurrying right along, Dot. Even now it will be late when we reach Mapletown. Your aunt and uncle won't know what has become of you."

The little girl climbed into the car again. Before they started, Mr. Elston reached into the back seat and picked up a square, pasteboard box.

"Here's a special treat for you," he said, taking off the lid.

"All-day-suckers!" cried Dot in delight. Never before had she seen so many except in the glass counter of a candy store. There were green, pink, red and yellow suckers, all fitted together in even rows.

"Help yourself," invited Mr. Elston cordially. "This box ought to keep you busy until we get to Mapletown."

Dot considered carefully before she made her selection. She chose a red sucker.

"Do you always travel with lollypops in your car?" she asked the man.

"Not always," he replied. "This happens to be a salesman sample."

During the ride back to Mapletown, Dot did not talk very much. She was too busy with the box of suckers. Mr. Elston didn't seem to care how many she had because he knew that each one would last a long while.

Soon it grew dark and the car lights were switched on.

"Curl up and go to sleep if you like," said Mr. Elston. "We still have a long drive ahead of us."

Dot tucked her feet up under her and laid

her head back on the cushioned seat.   In
a few minutes she was asleep.

A long while later the car stopped with a
bump as the wheels struck a cement curbing.   The little girl opened her eyes.

"Where are we now?" she asked drowsily.

"Mapletown," replied Mr. Elston as he
gave her a gentle shake.   "Wake up, Dot!
We'll find your aunt and uncle now, but it's
not going to be easy."

CHAPTER XV

A Prize for Aunt Betty

Mr. Elston helped Dot from the car and Dash leaped out beside them.

"It will be hard to locate your folks in this crowd," said the man, frowning.

Dot looked about then and saw that the car had been parked near the square. The streets were not as crowded as they had been during the day, but there were still a great many people in Mapletown.

Mr. Elston took Dot by the hand and led her into a corner drugstore. First he talked with the owner and then he went to the telephone and called several places. It took him so long that Dot sat down on a high stool to wait. She was getting sleepy again.

Finally, Mr. Elston came back.

"Well, I've reported you to the 'lost and found' committee," he said with a smile.

196

"Your aunt and uncle have been searching for you all afternoon."

"I hope they weren't worried," Dot replied.

"Well, they were—plenty. The difficulty now is that your aunt and uncle seem to be lost."

"Lost?" echoed Dot blankly.

"Well, not really. They're out somewhere on the streets looking for you. I'll take you over to one of the buildings. Sooner or later your folks will find you there."

Dot hoped that it would be very soon, for she was so tired. She wanted to lie down and go to sleep.

Mr. Elston led the little girl across the square to a large white building.

"Why, this is where they have all the sirup!" Dot exclaimed. "Aunt Betty has some of hers here!"

"It's also the place where lost children are left," said Mr. Elston as they went inside.

"Would you like to see Aunt Betty's sirup?" Dot invited. "I'll show it to you."

She led the man down the aisle. Aunt Betty's entry had been placed toward the north wall. Dot remembered the place.

"Here it is," she said proudly. "Someone has tied a ribbon on it. I guess maybe Aunt Betty thought it looked prettier that way."

"Why, it's the blue ribbon!" exclaimed Mr. Elston. "The judges awarded it to your aunt. She's won first prize!"

"Oh, I'm so glad!" cried Dot. "Does the ribbon mean her sirup is the very best?"

"Yes, it does, Dot. But you and I both knew it was good even before the judges gave her a ribbon."

"Oh, yes—" Dot completely forgot what she intended to say, for coming through the door, she saw Aunt Betty. Uncle Jack was only a few steps behind.

"Aunt Betty! Aunt Betty!" the little girl cried and ran to her.

"Oh, Dot!" murmured the woman and hugged her tightly. "Thank goodness, we've found you at last." Tears streamed down Aunt Betty's plump cheeks.

"No, we found *you!*" the little girl corrected.

Mr. Elston came up and explained how Dot had been carried away in his car. He told Aunt Betty too that he was sorry to have taken her sirup without waiting to pay for it.

"It doesn't matter now," said Aunt Betty. She had not listened very closely to what the man said. "You brought Dot back to us."

"The little girl has had quite an adventure," Mr. Elston declared. "But in a way it's lucky for all of us that she fell asleep in my car. Otherwise, I might never have found your place again."

"Don't worry about the sirup, sir," said Uncle Jack politely. "You've more than repaid the debt."

"Oh, no," said Mr. Elston, "but I intend to do so. You see I am a salesman for a large wholesale grocery firm. My duties include a certain amount of buying as well."

By this time both Uncle Jack and Aunt Betty were listening intently.

"I have been commissioned to place a large order for maple sirup. Wishing to get the very best for my firm, I went from place to place buying up samples for testing. I was in a great hurry when I stopped at your farm. I had no money with me except a ten dollar bill or I should have left change for the sirup."

"We didn't give it much thought," said Aunt Betty. "Dot worried more than anyone else. I guess she thought she hadn't tended the stand properly."

"How did our sirup test?" Uncle Jack inquired politely.

"Very highly. I have decided to place my order with the winner of the blue ribbon."

"Oh," murmured Aunt Betty, trying not to look disappointed.

"Why, that's you, Aunt Betty!" Dot cried. "You won the blue ribbon!"

"I did!" exclaimed Aunt Betty. "Oh, no, it can't be!"

"The little girl is right," smiled Mr. Elston. "Your sirup has been awarded first prize."

Even then Aunt Betty couldn't believe the good news until she went to look at the ribbon for herself.

"I declare, I'm happy enough to cry," she murmured. "Dot is safe, and now this piece of good luck!"

"All afternoon we've been combing the streets for Dot," Uncle Jack explained to Mr. Elston. "We forgot about the prize awards."

"This good fortune makes up for all our worry and anxiety," Aunt Betty added.

"I hope we'll be able to come to some agreement about the sirup," Mr. Elston said a trifle anxiously. "If you care to sell your entire output my firm will pay you a good price."

"You want all of our sirup?" gasped Aunt Betty.

"Yes, we'll probably need more than you have for sale."

Both Aunt Betty and Uncle Jack were so pleased that they couldn't keep from showing it. Always before they had sold their sirup a gallon at a time.

"It's a deal!" declared Uncle Jack heartily. "Come out to the house tomorrow and we'll arrange all the details."

He then wrote his name and address on a paper so that Mr. Elston would not forget where the farm was located.

Suddenly Dot plucked at her uncle's coat sleeve.

"Where is Dash?" she asked, trying to keep her voice steady. "He was here just a minute ago and now he's *gone*. He's lost, Uncle Jack!"

"I can't stand any more," murmured Aunt Betty. "If we have to spend the rest of the night hunting that dog—"

"That's not the pup over there?" asked Mr. Elston.

"Where?" cried Dot eagerly.

Then she saw that the man was looking at a curious ball of fur curled up under one of the counters.

"Why, it is Dash!" she cried in relief. "He must have crawled under there because he was so tired."

"Even Dash has had too big a day," declared Uncle Jack as he picked up the dog. "Let's be starting home before anyone else is lost."

During the ride back to the farm, Dash went off to sleep again, but Dot did not feel drowsy. She kept thinking over the many nice things which had happened that day.

"Oh, Uncle Jack!" she cried suddenly. "Mr. Elston forgot again!"

"Forgot what, child?" asked Aunt Betty.

"Why, the two dollars he promised to pay us for the sirup! He was to keep the money for me so it wouldn't be lost."

"That's right," agreed Uncle Jack. "But we'll not worry about a mere two dollars now. Through Mr. Elston Aunt Betty and I will be able to sell all of our sirup at a fine price."

"One never knows when bad luck will turn to good," declared Aunt Betty. "If Mr. Elston hadn't run off with the can of sirup, and if Dot hadn't been lost and climbed into his car—why, we'd have missed all this good fortune."

"I hope Mr. Elston doesn't forget his promise," Uncle Jack said a trifle anxiously. "I'll be glad when everything is arranged."

Dot was worried too for fear Mr. Elston might not come to the farm. But the very next day he arrived and asked Uncle Jack to sign certain papers. Everyone felt relieved then, for it meant that all of the maple sirup would be sold at a good price.

The following days were pleasant ones for Dot and Dash. The weather grew warm and they spent many hours out-of-doors. One morning the little girl watched Jeff spade a flower bed for Aunt Betty. She liked the smell of the fresh earth and Dash liked still better to dig in it.

Aunt Betty planted long rows of flowers along the walk.

"Well, it won't be long until summer will be here," she declared, wiping her grimy hands on her apron. "The tree leaves are coming out fast."

Dot hadn't realized that summer was so near. She sat down on the steps and for a long while didn't say anything.

During the warm months one could have so much fun in Fremont. It had been jolly living in Vermont, but she wanted to see Roger again, and the peacock. For days now she hadn't received any word from her parents. It worried her.

"Aunt Betty," she asked, "do you think there will be a letter for me today?"

"I hope so, child," Aunt Betty replied.

Dot began to watch anxiously for the mailman. When she saw him coming she rushed down to the gate. He smiled and waved to her but went right past.

Aunt Betty tried to cheer the little girl.

"Dot, do you know what day tomorrow will be?" she asked brightly.

"Why, it's Wednesday," Dot replied. "And I'll be seven years old!"

She had not thought that Aunt Betty knew about her birthday.

"How would you like to have a little party, Dot?"

"Oh, that would be wonderful, Aunt Betty! I hope Mary comes. We can have a lot of fun, then."

Mary did come, and a dozen other little girls who traveled a long way to reach the farm. They played games and Aunt Betty served a fine dinner with a large white cake bearing seven candles.

Dot had a very nice time but she kept thinking about her mother and father. It was her first birthday without them. She was afraid she might be getting a little bit homesick.

After the guests were gone, Dot saw a strange car rolling up the side road. It was painted yellow and on the door were the printed words: "Taxi."

Dot scarcely could believe her own eyes when she saw the two persons who were in the rear seat of the car.

"Why, it's Mother and Daddy!" she cried.

She rushed down to the road and flung herself into their arms.

"Oh, Dot, we've missed you so much," said Mother. She kissed the little girl several times and held her tight.

"I've missed you too," replied Dot. "And Daddy!"

The doctor lifted her right out of her mother's arms and perched her up on his broad shoulder.

"Mother has been ill," he said. "You are too heavy for her to hold."

"Isn't Mother cured yet?" the little girl asked anxiously.

"Oh, yes," her father replied, "but she must be careful not to overdo for a few weeks. In another month she'll be as strong as ever."

"We'll have lots of fun together," promised Mother. "I'm so eager to do things again."

Dot was very happy then. She laughed and talked and tried to tell her parents about everything that had happened to her while they had been away.

Dash scampered around the car but no one paid any attention to him. Then he jumped up on Mrs. Davidson, soiling her dress with his dirty paws.

"Oh, Mother, he wants you to say hello to him!" Dot cried.

Mrs. Davidson stooped down and patted Dash on the head, gently taking his paws from her gown.

"Has he been a good dog, Dot?" she asked.

"Oh, yes, real good for him, Mother. He sits up and speaks for me now, and he'll roll over too."

Mother and Daddy took a suitcase from the taxi cab and several large packages. They had not forgotten that it was Dot's birthday. Imogene received a new doll buggy, and there was a complete outfit for Dot—shoes, purse, coat, hat, and a little dress.

Mother and Daddy rested for several days. Then one morning Dot was awakened earlier than usual. They were to leave for Fremont that day.

"We'll hate to lose Dot," declared Aunt Betty as she saw the luggage being loaded into the car. "Next year you must all come back to Vermont for another long visit with us."

Goodbyes were said, and the car rolled slowly down the hill.

Dot kept looking back until the farmhouse was hidden from view. Through the woods she still could catch a glimpse of the old sugar house. In a moment it too would be gone.

A little lump came into Dot's throat. She felt as if she were saying farewell to some one very dear.

Then Dash joggled her arm with his wet little nose and sniffed. Dot was not quite sure what he was trying to say. She imagined he was telling her not to worry—next year they would return again to spend many happy hours among the magic maples.

THE END